School Daze

by

Robin Winberg

School Daze
Author: Robin Winberg
Copyright © April 2008

Disclaimer

In no way does this novel advocate school violence. It is the writer's personal belief that there are two sides to every story, and both sides need to be told and understood in order for a complete picture to be perceived.

We may all be familiar with the devastation and chaos left in the wake of every school disaster. However, do we really truly understand what provoked these individuals into performing such heinous acts against their classmates? I, for one, am willing to try a variety of new techniques if it will help alleviate this tragic plight that has befallen us.

Manufactured in the United States of America

ISBN: 978-0-6152-0072-9

Cover design by Chris Soyka

In Loving Memory of Louis John Ketchen

November 9, 1926 – October 1, 2008

Ja Che Koham, Dziadzi

To Shadow and Sera:

> *For showing me what really matters at the end of the day. I will always love and cherish you both for the wisdom you have bestowed on me and the unconditional love you have given me.*

Chapter 1

"Oops!" A jock said as he slammed his shoulder into mine. My books went flying out of my hands and spilled down the hallway. The jock and his friends kept walking, laughing as they exited.

Wonderful, I thought to myself as I bent down to pick up my books. Out of nowhere, a foot kicked my books further down the hall.

"Move freak. You're blocking my locker." A cheerleader sneered. She turned her attention to her locker and I knew that discussion was over.

I just sighed and continued to crawl down the hallway to scoop up my books. As I reached for my biology book, the bell rang. I sighed again. I knew that bell meant that I was going to be late for my English class.

Great, this is just what I need. I stood up, balancing myself against a locker. Looking down the hall I could see that most of the cattle herd had scattered, except for a few remaining stragglers. That meant if a hall monitor saw me, I would be an easy target for a tardy slip.

My heart started pounding as I sprinted down the corridor. With each passing step, the drums echoed louder and louder in my ears. The lava churned in my stomach, threatening to erupt at any second. My nerves were raw, seething at every second of existence. I was so nervous. What if I got stopped in the hallway? What if I received a tardy slip? That would be my third one. I would receive detention!

Once I had arrived at my destination, I graciously took a deep sigh of relief. Holding my head up, I opened the door and walked on an air of confidence inside my haven for the moment.

"You're late again, Robin." Mrs. Grant said. I could see a disapproving glare perched behind her glasses.

"I'm sorry, Mrs. Grant. I dropped my books." I quickly rushed to my seat as 44 eyes followed my every move.

"I'm sorry, too. See me after class." The teacher continued with her lecture, barely phased by what had transpired.

Those 4 words replayed in my head all throughout class. *See me after class*. It felt like a worm was wiggling inside my head. *See me after class*. What was she going to say? What was going to happen? I had no idea, but I knew in my gut that it wasn't good.

I stared at my notebook most of the time, occasionally looking up to see what she was writing on the board. Not that it mattered. Not that I wrote any of it down.

When the bell rang, I looked up at Mrs. Grant. Without missing a cue, my heart started to throw itself against my ribcage, demanding to be released. Like a dog caught red handed, I gathered my things and slowly walked over to her desk. Blinking, I raised my head and our eyes locked.

"Recently, you've been coming late to my class. Is something going on that I should know about?" Mrs. Grant's voice echoed with concern. For a split second I wanted to tell her how every day, the same cheerleader kicked my books down the hallway. In the end, I just bit my tongue.

"No Mrs. Grant, I'm sorry. I'll try and get here on time." I said, my voice barely above a sorrowful whisper.

Shaking her head, the teacher wrote out a hall pass. With the grace of an expert ballerina, her arm extended. I accepted the pass.

As I walked to my next class, resent began coursing through my veins. *Why didn't I just tell her what was going on?* I pondered, weighing the consequences. Should I tell someone that the cheerleaders got their daily kicks by torturing me, or should I bite my tongue and hold my silence?

"No!" I said viciously. "I will NOT be treated like this. I'm not doing anything to them, and there is no reason that they should do this to me!" With a new determination, I turned around. I felt renewed energy pumping through my veins.

Upon arrival to Mrs. Grant's door, the ghosts of education days past caught up with me. He whispered repressed memories in my ears, and I knew he was speaking the truth.

One fall day, many years ago, a shy and tiny brunette entered the play area in her kindergarten class. It was the beginning of October in 1997, and recess just began.

I sat on a swing, gleefully kicking my problems away. How I loved those swings. It didn't matter what happened the rest of the day. For that hour, I was a million miles away, up in the air, in my own little universe.

I was so far away that I didn't see the hand reach out and grab the swing to an abrupt stop until it was too late. My universe came crashing to a halt, and the momentum propelled me to a crashing stop on the ground.

My hand rushed to my face. My nose burned, spewing blood. I turned around to gaze at my nemesis.

His name was Matt, and he stood next to the swing. His hand was still on the rope; a smile graced his face.

"It's my turn to swing." His dimples regally stared down at me, and his evil eyes showed a carnal delight in my pain.

I got up, running to a teacher. Tears ran down my face, trying to outrace the blood. Concern filled the attendants' faces, and the hens (amongst all their clucking) quickly ushered me to the nurses' office.

As soon as the blood flow had slowed to a trickle, my mother and the principal entered the room.

"Honey! What happened?!" My mother did little to hide the panic in her voice. I started crying. Reaching my arms up, I wanted to be back in my own little world and escape the horrors of reality. Mom wrapped her arms around me, shielding me as best she could.

"Mommy, it was awful! I was swinging, and someone grabbed the rope! The swing stopped, but I didn't. I landed on my face!" I blurted out in between sobs.

"Do you know who grabbed the rope, Robin?" A gently masculine voice whispered. I knew it was the principal, Mr. Theodore.

"Yes." I sniffled. My outpour of emotion was coming to an end, even though my soul had been slashed raw with pain. "It was Matt. He's a boy in my class."

"The one that said you were ugly and spit gum in your hair last week?" Mom asked incredulously. I nodded.

My mother and the principal exchanged looks, and I knew something was going to be said in private. I didn't know what either was thinking, but I could tell from the expressions on their faces that neither adult was happy.

I waited in the nurses' office while they went to Mr. Theodore's office. I don't know what was discussed, but I know that when Mom came back, she took me home.

The next day, Matt wasn't in class. I was happy that I didn't have to see him. That is, I was happy until lunch.

The three hours between the start of school and lunch had lulled me into a false sense of security. I had just gotten comfortable in my safety when I opened my lunch pail. Somebody had put live worms in it.

I screamed and threw my lunch pail, spilling the contents everywhere. Panic grabbed me, shaking me violently. The other kids however, thought it was hilarious. They began to laugh at my expense.

While no one admitted to doing it, I knew why it was done. Someone put worms in my lunch pail as retribution for Matt being suspended.

From that day on, I remained curled up inside my own little world. I rarely fought back because I knew that defending myself (or anyone defending me) would mean there would be more consequences. No matter the battle or the battlefield, I would never win. I COULD never win.

My breath escaped my lips, and sadness replaced the air inside me with the ease of an Olympic gymnast. As I stood outside Mrs. Grant's door, I knew that I couldn't say anything. Yes, saying something would feel good right now, but those smug little bastards would feel justified in launching another attack. And I was tired of being attacked.

Turning around, my head dropped to my shoulders as I retreated back to the corridor of doom. Half sulking, half dragging myself, I started my journey towards biology lab.

Thoughts swirled inside my head of possibilities. Would they throw a frog at me? Maybe more worms. I didn't know. But whatever my peers were going to do, they were going to do it. *Might as well get it over with before lunch.*

Upon entering the lab, everyone hushed as I walked in. Mrs. Johnson turned around from her position at the chalkboard in time to see me drop the hall pass on her desk. Mrs. Johnson was an older woman who was of equal proportions. You know, as wide as she was tall. Her skin was as white as her hair, which she always kept in the same bun. Her glasses were petite, resting on the small bump on the middle of her nose. She always wore these weird flower print dresses, which were wrinkle free. Just like her facial expressions. Wrinkle free, always in control.

Without missing a beat or saying a word, I dashed to my seat and curled up inside of it. *I wish they'd stop staring at me*, I thought to myself. *Can't you asses find something more exciting than torturing someone else*? I could feel their eyes on me. Even worse, I could feel their evil smiles aimed at me.

As time went by, I lost myself in taking notes. So lost, I didn't even notice that class was almost over. Looking at the clock, there was 2 minutes left before the bell rang for lunch.

"Robin. Are you listening to me?" Mrs. Johnson asked.

"Huh?" I replied at the sound of my name. The other kids snickered.

"Please stay a minute after class. I would like to speak with you." The irritation began to rise up in her voice. I only nodded a reply.

Mrs. Johnson wrote the assignment due on the board before the bell rang. Once that sound echoed, all of the cattle resumed its herd like motion towards the corridors.

I didn't move.

Sashaying over to me, Mrs. Johnson sat down in the seat next to me.

"Is anything going on Robin?" Mrs. Johnson spoke softly. I was unable to tell which emotion she was feeling. That made me nervous. If I answered wrong, I could start problems. And problems with the faculty were something I definitely wanted to avoid.

"No. Why would you think there are problems?" I asked innocently. The way I saw it, innocence was one of the responses that would cause the least chance of a hostile situation.

"Well, for starters, you're almost never late to my class. And for second, it's not like you to not pay attention." Mrs. Johnson listed.

"Sorry I was late. Mrs. Grant wanted to talk to me for a minute. She wanted to know why I carry my books instead of putting them in my bag." I smiled.

"Okay. That answers my first question. What about my second question?"

"Sorry. I just wanted the notes I was writing to be complete and thorough, but neat enough to read when I got home. I HATE taking notes if you can't read them later. Then it's like, what's the point of taking notes if you can't read them?" I tried to sound cheerful. I knew I was babbling. I babbled when I was nervous. Luckily, the teacher didn't know that.

Judging by her expression, she bought it. I smiled at her. She smiled back.

"Okay. As long as nothing is wrong." She slowly nodded in approval.

"Anything else?" I asked.

"Are you in a hurry?" Mrs. Johnson questioned.

"No, because I have lunch next. I just don't want to go to my locker and get stopped in the hallways during lunch. I'd get in trouble that way!" I smiled again. I was getting so cheerful that I wanted to slap myself!

"Good point. Go ahead Robin. And don't forget. Quiz on Monday." Mrs. Johnson rose from her seat. I followed suit, rising up moments behind her.

"See you tomorrow!" I said over my shoulder, rushing out the door.

Running towards my locker, I could feel raw power pulsing through my veins. This was lunch. I could go anywhere during lunch. Lunch was my time, where I could find a hole to curl up in and escape from the wiles of reality. Nobody could bother me. None of the other students cared enough to bother me during lunch. Lunch was also their time, and they

spent more effort socializing with each other than destroying my self

esteem. Any reprieve was a blessing, and every day, I was continually

grateful. I let every possible entity in the hierarchy of ultimate power

know it.

****

This was a typical day at high school for me. It wasn't a matter of

being able to succeed at my classes. It had nothing to do with hanging out

with friends. All I was trying to do was survive, and it seemed that I was

failing.

The rest of my day went similar to the morning's events. I kept my

attention focused on being able to go home after school. Home. The safest

place I knew of. I knew that when I got home, I would be able to indulge

in my most secret of pleasures.

cheerleaders walking down the hallway. My auditory sense told me they were snickering.

The pain was intense. It was on the top of my left eye socket, at the bone. While it was bone, it was still a very tender part of the body. The heat that emanated off of the swelling was intense. Through no control of my own, my vision became blurry with excess blood flow and tears.

Damn it, I thought to myself. *Don't cry. Come on, Robin. Don't cry. Son of a bitch! What is her problem?*

I knew it was the same damn cheerleader that always kicked my books down the hallway. The only thing I didn't know was the future. What was I going to say? I knew people would ask about my eye. I knew it would swell, and it would bruise. What was I going to say that would explain it?

I was furious, and sighing with exasperation was the only thing I would do right now. Besides that, I knew I needed to 'treat' my would-be black eye. Sighing, I raised myself up to a slightly hunched caveman position. Throwing most of my weight into it, I swung my book bag over my right shoulder and headed down the hallway to the nurses' office.

Upon my arrival, I gently knocked at the door. My rapture stirred no movement. Part of me wished the nurse was at lunch, and the other part of me wished that she would usher me into her office with TLC and help me take care of this 'problem'.

I decided to knock a second time. This time I knocked louder. Still, no answer.

Sighing, I turned around and headed back down the hallway. The best thing I could think to do was to go to a bathroom and put cold water on it.

With my head down, I sulked down the hallways. The only things I could think of were, *How am I going to explain this?* and *Why did she do that?* and *I hope I don't run into someone. I don't want to get caught 'roaming' the halls and get detention.*

Luckily for me, the halls were as desolate as the souls of my peers. Cautiously, I turned every corner.

After 78 agonizing seconds, I pushed the door to the lavatory open. Peeking in with my good eye told me that I was alone.

I rushed over to the sink. With one hand, I checked to make sure the water was running cold. With the hand that was covering my eye, I threw paper towels into the sink. My right hand grabbed up the paper towels and levitated them up to the water.

While the water was soaking the towels, I gazed up at the mirror. There was a large red lump that pushed my eye partially shut. Inside that lump was a gash (I assume that's where I made contact with the edge of the locker). The lump was reddish and bluish and purplish. It was dark, and bright, and intense. Worst of all, it was very noticeable.

Stopping the water, I flopped the cold wet towels on my face. I didn't care they were soaked. I didn't bother to waste time wringing them out. I let the water drip wherever it may have.

Just in time, too. Senior hens clucked into the bathroom, staring strangely at me. I offered a fake smile.

"I got something in my eye." I said.

My statement didn't illicit a response. Just more strange stares.

Great, I thought. *Well, fine. Don't care. Just go about your merry little business and leave me alone.*

Sighing again (for what seemed the millionth time that day), I threw the paper towels away as I walked out the door.

Within seconds, I could feel the heat radiate off of the 'lump'. My stride grew longer as my anger grew hotter. I was pissed and getting more pissed by the footstep. Didn't anybody care? Some BITCH pushed me into my locker, and nobody cared! I mean, honestly. How could someone look at another person and know something was wrong, and not care? Is that what this world had come to?

Making a rash decision, I stormed back up to my locker. Ripping it open, I tossed my book bag in it. Gathering what I needed, I closed the door. I had decided to walk home. I wasn't going to stay in this school another minute. Not today. Today, I was done. At that moment, no one or nothing could make me stay. And I was determined to escape.

5 minutes to spare before the bell rang and I slinked out the side door. Without a sound, I scaled the back hills of the school. Lucky for me, I lived 10 minutes away from the high school. Lucky and unlucky, I suppose.

The whole walk home, I kept my head down. My mind was completely blank the whole walk home. I didn't care. I knew I would deal with repercussions from this. I also knew that my eye would become a topic of discussion, whether I wanted to talk about it or not. Despite the unhappy

events to come, I desperately sought solace. And that was why I walked

home that day.

Once I reached the end of my road, I ran the rest of the way home.

Pulling open my door, I flung myself inside and ran upstairs to my room.

Turning on my computer, I loaded a writing program and began to vent.

October 09, 2006   12:19pm

I know. This entry is kind of early. I'm sorry. I couldn't stand it anymore! You should see my eye! It's awful. That same cheerleader pushed me into my locker. Now it's all black and blue. I know mom's going to want to talk about it when she gets home. I'll just tell her I tripped and fell and hurt myself. She'll believe I did. God, I wish something bad would happen to that bitch. What the hell is her problem? I've never done anything to her. I hope she cracks her head open. Then everyone can see she hasn't got the brains she should and put her in a zoo! I think I'm going to go take a nap. And mom said "High school is the best years of your life." I've only been a freshman at Fox Grove High School for a month, and already my life sucks!

Chapter 3

The sounds of creaky cabinets and tip toes echoed, delicately caressing my ear drums. Slowly, I stirred. I knew those sounds meant Mom was in the kitchen. I also knew I had no desire to get up. As cognitive thought slowly began to show function, I realized how much of the day my nap had consumed. Had I really slept almost 6 hours? Rolling over, I could see the day glow eyes of my alarm clock. It read 5:53pm. Wow. I guess I had.

Fumbling around in the dark, I grabbed my feetie pajamas and put them on. Navigating in the dark, I eventually made my way downstairs.

"So there you are," my mom's voice sounded less than chipper. "Where have you been hiding?"

"I took a nap," I replied. My voice was quiet. I was still groggy.

"You and those darn pajamas. Aren't you too big for them yet?" Mom's voice resonated with amusement.

"Never!" My voice boomed, raising an arm in triumph. I loved my feetie pajamas. You know, the kind little kids wear with the feet still attached? One of the perks of being a 'runt', I guess. It meant I didn't have to give up certain things I liked from my childhood. Not that being a runt was a bad thing. Being smaller than 85% of people meant I didn't hit my head on things, I could fit in more places, and there was a larger selection of clothes that I could fit into (since I could still fit into the kids' section).

I wasn't too terribly small. Just smaller than most of the other people I came into contact with. As a freshman, I was 5'1" and 71lbs (soaking wet), so it wasn't hard for other people to beat me in a competition of 'who's bigger?'

I had temporarily forgotten about the incident that transcribed at lunch earlier, so I was completely startled when my mother grabbed me by my shoulders and spun me around to face her.

"Robin Rachael! Where the hell did that come from?" Anger and concern could distinctly be heard in my mother's words. It took me a second to figure out what she was talking about.

"I tripped at school mom. I fell into my locker. It's no big deal." I mumbled, trying to wiggle out of her grasp. All efforts were an exercise in futility, for I couldn't escape.

"So why do I not believe you?" Mom pressed on.

I shrugged.

"Maybe because you have never looked me in my eyes and lied to my face. And when you told me that you tripped, you were staring at the floor."

Gazing up, I could see that she had an air of "I know I'm right" written in the twinkles of her eyes. Damn it. I had no choice but to tell her the truth.

Sighing, I looked her straight in the eyes. "I was in my locker at lunch. I was getting my afternoon books out and putting my morning books away when a cheerleader pushed me into my locker."

"Why would she do a thing like that?" My mother asked incredulously.

"I don't know, but she's always kicking my books down the hallway in the morning. That's why I'm always late to English. Her locker's next to mine. She says that I take up too much space so she can't get into hers." My heart broke as I told her the truth. It was painful talking about the ordeals that I endured.

After a pause my mother asked gently, "Do you know her name?"

I shook my head. "No, but her locker number is 314. It's on the left side of mine."

Nodding, mom slowly released me from her hold. Taking a step back, she turned and walked towards her purse.

"Where are you going, mom?" I asked.

"Nowhere, honey. I'm going to make a phone call." Mom took out her cell phone and waited impatiently for the other person to pick up.

I could hear a mumble of a male's voice on the other line. "Hello, Mr. Petersen? It's me, Annie. I was wondering if I could speak with you in your office in the morning."

Oh, crap. Mom had called Mr. Petersen, the superintendent of Fox Grove School District. My stomach immediately knotted up, threatening to obey its nervous master. Damn it. I knew that there were going to be repercussions from this. There always were. That's what I got for having a mother who was on the PTA board. She had the superintendent on speed dial.

"We're going to see Mark at 10am, ok sweetie?" Mom said as soon as she shut her phone. I just blinked at her, staring.

"What's wrong?"

"What if the other cheerleaders get mad at me for saying anything?" I asked, worried.

"They won't honey. You didn't do anything wrong. You never hit that cheerleader, so she had no reason to hit you." Mom said matter-of-fact.

"I know but it's not like that in high school, mom. It's worse." The worry began to resonate more and more with every breath.

"Listen. Take it or leave it. I'm taking you to the doctors' tomorrow morning, and then we're going to meet with Mark." Mom began shuffling around the kitchen, gathering miscellaneous ingredients for an unknown dinner.

"Wait. What? Why are we going to the doctor's?" I asked, surprised.

"Because that eye looks awful. I want to make sure there's no permanent damage or anything's broken."

Walking over to mom's purse, I dug around for her compact. I knew she always carried a mirror with her. I hadn't taken a look at it since the bathroom. I wondered how bad it got.

With a flicker of movement, I heard the clasp pop. I opened the compact and gazed into my reflection.

I saw what made mom gasp. I saw what got her upset. Although my eye wasn't as warm as it was upon initial contact, it was an array of colors. Most of all, it was massively swollen.

Below the bone, just under my eyebrow, was a cut. The cut was deep and oozed a mix of blood and clear liquid. It was an inch and a half long, with a diameter of a half inch. Surrounding the cut, the colors radiated outward. First up was a dark purple. The next layer of color was a lesser purple, but purple nonetheless. And finally, the last color of the bruise was red before my skin resumed its natural hues. The size resembled the area of a baseball.

Strange, I thought. *I can still see out of it*. It hadn't occurred to me prior to thinking about it that I could still retain function over my bodily abilities. I wasn't "impaired" by this to any degree.

Throughout dinner, my thought swirled around the possibility of "the backlash." I was thinking about what the cheerleader's friends would do in retaliation when my mother's voice penetrated my thoughts.

"You've hardly touched your food." Mom spoke gently.

"I'm sorry mom." I sighed.

"What's wrong?" She asked.

"I told you. I don't want the cheerleader to do anything about me talking to the superintendent."

"She won't. She has no right to. She's wrong for hurting you, especially since you never do anything to her. And if she or someone she knows lashes out because of this, she's only making things worse for herself."

Sighing again, my worry and irritation began to show. "I know mom, but it doesn't mean it won't happen. Remember what happened in kindergarten? Even though Matt was wrong for pushing me off the swing and I got hurt, his friends still put worms in my lunchbox. It didn't matter then if I was right and they were wrong, and it's not going to matter now."

As soon as I said it, I was sorry. But it didn't matter. It was how I felt. For some reason, I still felt guilty. I looked down at my food.

She reached over and rubbed my shoulder. "Listen honey. I know it's hard. And I know that the other kids are mean and they blame you. They're immature. That's why they don't accept responsibility for their own actions. It doesn't excuse their poor behavior. It just helps you understand where they're coming from."

"What about where I'm coming from, Mom?" I asked.

"What about it?"

"Well, you're telling me to understand where they're coming from, but they don't take the time to understand where I'm coming from. I don't think that's fair. I think they should reciprocate, don't you?" I lifted my gaze and met hers.

"Yes I do. Unfortunately, the world doesn't work like that. I wish it did. If you want, you can tell me where you're coming from, because I'd like to know." Mom smiled. Her smile was always infectious. It spread, and it didn't matter what you were feeling. You couldn't help but smile back.

"Okay. Well, it makes me angry when that cheerleader kicks my books down the hallway every day. I never do anything to her. I don't even know her name. I don't know if she knows mine. I don't know why she kicks my books down. She says they're in her way and that's why she does it every day. But she didn't say a word to me when she shoved me into my locker. I knew it was her though. I turned around and looked and saw her laughing with her friends." I paused, looking at my mom's reaction. She appeared thoughtful, as if absorbing everything. I proceeded.

"I don't know. I just wish that everyone would leave me alone. I go to my classes, I take notes, I don't talk to anyone, and I just go there and do what I have to do. I've never hit anyone in school. So why do they think its okay to hit me? Do they think it's funny? Do they think its okay since I won't hit back? But then, how would they feel if someone did it to them?" At this point I was rambling. I didn't care. It felt good to get it all out.

"Well, make sure you tell Mark what you told me. Just try not to sound emotional when you tell him. If you tell him what you told me like you're presenting facts, he'll be much more receptive to you." Mom rubbed my shoulder again.

"Are you going to call me in tomorrow morning, mom?" I asked. I knew I had to ask her about the "half day" I took off.

"Yes I am. Why?" she returned my question with a question.

"I was just wondering. Hey mom, I was wondering something." Now or never, I thought. I might as well get it over with.

"What's that?"

"Could you write me a note for today?" I gave her a guilty smile. You know the kind I mean. Where you pull the corners of your mouth up, but your eyes say, "uh oh."

"Why would you need a note for today?" Mom asked, giving me a disapproving motherly look.

"Well, like I said. The cheerleader pushed me into my locker at lunch time. So right after it happened, I went to the nurses' office. But no one was there. So I went to the bathroom and put cold water on it. And then a few seniors walked in and started looking at me like I had two heads. So I got really upset and went home." At the end, my voice got really quiet. I knew it was wrong of me, and it wasn't fair of me to ask her to bail me out. But a part of me just wanted this crap to go away.

Mom sighed. "I'll think about it. But you know you shouldn't have walked home. You should've gone right to the principals' office. Or the main office to call me. Just because things get hard, it doesn't mean you can walk out. You know that, Robin."

"I know. I'm sorry, mom." I spoke softly.

****

And that was our dinner conversation. After dinner, I just went to my room and played solitaire on my computer. It seemed like an eternity until I heard footsteps coming up the stairs. Turning towards the door, I watched for any sign of movement. I wondered if my mother was going to peek her head in. Did she have anything to say? Was there anything on her mind?

"Good night," I called out.

"Good night honey. Get some sleep." Mom replied before shutting her door.

All night I lay in bed, watching the hours slowly creep past me. The last time I noticed the clock saying was 2:43am. It was so hard to sleep. I was so nervous about the meeting with Mark. What was going to come of it?

Rather than lay in bed awake, I decided to hop on my computer. If I wasn't going to sleep, then I could at least write in my journal.

October 10, 2006   2:46am

Damn it! Mom saw my eye. She called the superintendent. I don't mind

that she made a big deal out of it. I'm just worried that other people are

going to make a big deal out of it. I don't want muss and fuss. I just want

everything to go calmly and smoothly. I just want peace. It's not like I'm

doing bad things to get attention. That's just it. I don't want attention!

Now I can't sleep. I'm so nervous about what's going to happen

tomorrow. I asked her about a note for missing my classes after lunch.

She's not sure. She said she'll think about it. I really hope she does. I don't

want detention for missing my classes. I feel bad about missing them, it's

just that I didn't want to deal with anything else that day. I don't know.

We'll have to see what happens I guess.

Chapter 4

The next morning was a circus of events, beginning with a trip to the doctors. I didn't think it was bad enough to seek out medical attention, but my mother insisted. Maybe she knew something I didn't. After all, isn't that how the saying goes? "Mother knows best?"

I wasn't too fond of the doctor's office. Actually, I had no qualms with the office itself. It was the poking and prodding and unnecessary touching by strangers that I detested.

Dr. Gohn gently touched my eye, applying pressure. I winced.

"Does this hurt?" He asked.

"Yes." I said, thinking, *Duh! Of course it hurts! Have you looked at it, or are you blind?!*

"How's your vision in this eye?" He asked with the same monotone note.

"Fine." I replied.

A couple mmhmms and hmmmms later, Dr. Gohn abandoned his brail reading of my face in favor of writing on his clipboard.

"So what's the verdict?" Mom asked.

"Well, as far as I can tell, there won't be any permanent damage. She didn't chip the bone. But she's lucky. A couple of centimeters lower, and she would've lost that eye completely. It's going to take some time to heal, but within a few months, she should be as good as new. Although I'd like to give her a tetanus shot. You said she hit her locker at school?" Dr. Gohn announced his findings.

"Yes, that's right. That's a good idea. I think she should get a tetanus shot too. I have no idea how old those lockers are." Mom nodded in agreement.

I gritted my teeth. I hated needles, but I knew it was an exercise in futility to argue. There was no way I was going to get away with NOT getting that shot.

I don't know if it's an immediate subconscious act or if it's because it's on your conscious mind, but as soon as the band aid had been applied, I furiously rubbed my wound.

"Are you ready, sweetie?" Mom asked.

"Yeah," I grumbled.

We hadn't made it very far through the lobby when a perky petite woman approached us. She looked vaguely familiar....

"Good morning, Anne. How are you doing today?" She said.

"Cindy! It's so nice to see you! To what do I owe the pleasure?" Mom smiled.

"Well, I'm the prosecutor assigned to your daughter's case. I was wondering if we could take some pictures as evidence and get the doctor's report. With your permission, of course." Cindy smiled back.

"Oh, absolutely!" Mom kept smiling. How could she smile about something so heinous? "Robin, you remember Cindy right?"

I returned her question with a blank expression.

"She was my lawyer when I divorced your father."

"Oh yeah. Hi," I said quietly.

"Hi honey. It's nice to see you again." Cindy quietly chirped. She stuck out her hand, waiting to shake mine. I obliged, hoping it would end the awkward moment.

"Shall we start taking pictures?" Cindy chirped again. Her perkiness was beginning to get on my nerves.

"Pictures of what?" I asked, immediately embarrassed when the stupidity of my question had left my mouth.

"Pictures of that eye. If we're going to prosecute the offender, we need evidence. And it'll be a good thing when that eye heals, but it wouldn't help our case." Cindy smiled. I smiled back.

"Anne, would it be okay if we got the doctor's report on this? That way we can use his medical expertise." Cindy asked Mom.

"We aren't going to need her father's involvement in this, are we?" Mom asked. She sounded concerned.

"No, we shouldn't. Has he had visitation with the child since the divorce?" Cindy asked.

"Nope." Mom replied.

"Has he paid child support?" Cindy asked again.

"Yes, but only because the court threatened to throw him in prison for violating the order."

"Do you have sole custody?" Cindy asked another question. There was no doubt that the killer instinct a lawyer had was still inside of her.

"Yes, I do. He never asks to visit her or see her or how she's doing or anything." Mom said sadly.

"Then, no. You are the only person we need to discuss the trial and your daughter with." Cindy said matter-of-factly.

The adults were back to their own conversation, one that didn't include anyone under the drinking age. The rest of the "meeting" went that way, with me sitting still long enough to endure a couple dozens snap shots and being quiet long enough to have the doctor tell Cindy what he told us. I just sighed, waiting to get this over with. The faster this meeting was done, the faster the meeting with the superintendent would be over with as well.

As they chatted, my mind wandered to reminiscing about my father. It had been almost a decade since I had seen him. He had left in favor of his secretary. I didn't really remember him, except for the absence and constant fighting. He was almost never home. And when he was, he would violently argue with mom about every little thing. It was horrible.

Every now and then, I thought about him. I wondered what he was doing, how he was, what became of him. I also wondered if he ever thought about me.

What little girl doesn't think about her daddy?

****

As we waited in the main lobby of Mark's office, my doctor's words replayed in my head. I couldn't believe it. Since my doctor talked to my mom about me (like I wasn't even there), it was hard to believe that he was even talking about me at all. "A couple of centimeters lower, and she would've lost that eye completely."

"Are you coming?" Mom asked. She was standing up. I could see Mark's head peering out of his office door. I lifted myself up and followed like an obedient dog. Keeping my head down, I watched her feet move. If they stopped, I stopped. If they moved, I moved.

"Have a seat, ladies." Mark said. For a man, he had a very gentle voice. In fact, the way his gaze caressed you made you feel cared about, as if the compassion he had in his heart were being shot through his eyes like lasers.

"Would you like to tell me what happened yesterday Robin?" Mark asked me.

I shrugged. "I guess." Slowly, quietly, I began to recount the events. I started with how I had stayed after in Mrs. Johnson's' class. I told him how I went to my locker after that to retrieve my afternoon books.

"And in the middle of pulling out my history book, I get pushed from behind. That's when my face hit the edge of the locker door. You know, where it comes in contact with the right edge of the locker. I looked down the hallway and saw a bunch of cheerleaders walking past me and laughing. I'm not sure which one pushed me, but I noticed the girl whose locker is next to mine was there. She has blonde cork screw curly hair. You can't miss it. It's very curly hair." I bobbed my head up and down, adamant about her hair. When I got nervous, that was another bad habit of mine. Focusing on trivial things as opposed to what was important. I couldn't help it! I was nervous!

Mark nodded, as if to say he had absorbed my words. "Well, thank you for telling me what happened yesterday, Robin. Could you excuse us for a minute please? You're welcome to go to the lounge and get a drink if you'd like."

"Thank you, Mr. Petersen. Enjoy the rest of your day." I gave Mark and my mom a fake smile, and left. I hated when adults talked without us around. It made me mad, and in this case, anxious. What did they talk about to each other that they couldn't talk about in front of us? Besides, it's not like I wasn't going to find out what was going to come of this meeting anyways. I sighed, and looked at the box of donuts sitting on the table. They looked yummy. I couldn't help myself.

"What are you doing in here?" A voice behind me asked. Turning around, I could see the receptionist staring at me. Wonderful. And I had just swiped one of her donuts.

Keeping my eyes on the ground, I replied, "My mom's still talking to Mr. Petersen. He told me to wait in here."

"Ahhh. Well, they might be awhile. Would you like me to make you some cocoa?" She smiled. I smiled back and nodded. Walking over to a cabinet, she removed two packets of cocoa. After she had prepared two cups, she handed one to me.

"Thank you," I replied, watching the freeze dried marshmallows swirl around.

"So, to what do we owe the pleasure of your visit?" She asked.

"Someone pushed me into my locker yesterday." I looked up, allowing her to get a good view of my eye. I blinked, as if to emphasize the damage.

She grimaced. "Oh lovely. Does it hurt?"

"A lot." I smiled. She smiled back.

"My name's Nancy." She extended her hand.

I took it in mine, shaking gently. "Hi, Ms. Nancy. My name's Robin."

Nancy and I chatted for a while. I didn't even notice how time had escaped me, but somewhere in our conversation, mom had appeared.

"Sorry that took so long, kiddo. Are you ready to go?" Mom tilted her head towards the right, looking at me like a dog who heard the word "car".

I glanced up at the clock. It read 12:10 pm. Somehow, somewhere, two hours had floated off into the distance of reality.

"Where are we going?" I asked. Common sense would've told me one of two places. Either she was taking me to school or taking me home. But sometimes words escaped mouths before brains could step in and say, "Now let's think about this scenario for a second, because logically we can come up with the answer."

"We're going home." She walked over to me and wrapped her arm around my shoulders.

"Have fun." Nancy smiled and walked away, no doubt back to her desk.

Mom and I scampered off towards the car, towards home. Part of me wanted to know what was said, what happened, what was going to happen, and a million of other questions. Part of me wanted to wait and see what mom had to say.

During the ride home, I kept looking at mom, but she didn't say anything. My heart pounded faster and faster, almost as if it wasn't circulating fast enough. It couldn't circulate fast enough. Faster and faster it went, until my hands shook from the force of my heart. Finally, after 5 minutes of silence and passing scenery, I couldn't take it any longer.

"So what did you two talk about?" I asked. My voice was shakier upon delivery than I had anticipated. I'm sure mom could tell I was nervous.

She sighed. Taking a deep breath, she answered, "Well, Mark isn't happy about this. In fact, he asked me if I wanted to press charges. It turns out the girl is 17. Since you're only 14, it's my decision to make on if I want to have her arrested."

I felt as if I had been slapped upside the head with a sandbag. I was in shock! I couldn't believe what my ears were telling me!

"Well? What are you going to do?" I pressed on, trying to obtain a full picture of what had transpired from her.

"What would you like me to do, honey?" Mom answered my question with a question.

"I don't know. You're the adult. You tell me. I'm just the minor!" I tried to lighten the mood with a silly answer. No smile out of mom.

"Well, I told Mark that I wanted that cheerleader removed from the school. At least move her locker away from yours. If she did it once, unprovoked, she'll do it again. And I'm not risking your other pretty eye looking that bad."

"Is she going to be arrested?" I asked. "Inquiring minds want to know."

"Yes, dear. She is. I told you, I'm not risking her or any other student attacking my baby. There is no reason for her to behave that way." Mom informed me.

"Do I need to talk to the police about what happened?"

"Maybe. You do need to be there so you can show them your eye. That way, they'll understand how bad it is."

"When are we going to do that?" I asked.

"Tomorrow. Right before the assembly."

"Assembly? What assembly?" I asked, partially frantic. I hated assemblies, but for the school to throw one that they hadn't planned was bad. If mom was telling me the truth, and I suspected she was, Mark had decided to have the police talk to all of the students about why it was bad. That meant that when the other cheerleaders saw their friend being arrested and MY eye, they were going to connect the two! Damn it!

"The assembly Mark is throwing to educate the students about how violence is unacceptable." Mom said. There was a certain determination in her voice, one that I heard very rarely. This was business. It was almost as if mom's voice was telling me what her words weren't. The message was simple: While what she was doing was the right thing, the war wasn't over. And it was going to get harder before it got better.

"Well, do you know exactly what the cops are going to say?" I asked. I wanted to know everything. I wanted to be prepared. My mind was reeling with information and possibilities. Maybe if I knew every little thing that the adults were planning, then I could interpret how my peers were going to react. And if I knew how they were going to react, then I could prepare the best defense for myself. That way, I didn't end up with another black eye.

"No, I don't dear. We'll just have to wait and see." Mom said.

"Are you going to be at the assembly?" I responded.

"I'm not sure yet. It depends if my boss will let me out of work in the afternoon so that I can make it." With that statement, the rest of the car ride was ridden in silence.

Once we pulled onto our street, I felt a calming wave wash over me. I knew that my sanctum sanctorum was nearby. When I got there, nothing bad could happen to me. Theoretically speaking, of course. When I saw my house, the left corner of my mouth pulled upwards. We were home.

Before the car's engine took an afternoon nap, I bounded out of the metal vestibule and inside the brick framework of happiness. All of the familiar sounds and smells greeted me upon entrance of my abode. I don't care who says what. Vacations may be nice, but it's the little things that you take for granted when you're home. And home is always where my heart will be.

Immediately, I retreated to my room. I had been handed a mass of information, and I had to figure out a way to wrap my mind around it. I had to analyze this from every angle. I had to think of a solution. Slowly, my computer awoke.

October 10, 2006 12:43 pm

Holy crap! So I saw the superintendent today. He's throwing a huge

assembly tomorrow. That's what mom says. I don't know. They talked for

two hours after I left the room. Personally, I would've liked to stay, seeing

as how it does involve me. I hate it when adults do that. They treat us like

we're inferior. We're not! Anyways, like I said, there's going to be a huge

assembly tomorrow. The cops are coming to talk to everyone about school

violence. Mom also decided to push charges on the girl that pushed me

into my locker. I'm glad. That bitch deserves to have her ass handed to

her. I never did anything to her! And I shouldn't have had this done to me!

Well, we'll see how she likes being punished. Hahaha. I wish she was here

right now. I'd laugh at her. I'd ask her how it feels to have her back

against a corner. Sucks, don't it? Although I'm worried about the

assembly. Will people think I'm a snitch? Will they know it's because of

me? I hope not. That would mean they're going to come after me again.

This time would be worse though. Because this time, they'd be mad. I

hope not. I just want to be left alone. I don't know. We'll see. I hope nobody is smart enough to put two and two together. If some people see

my eye and they noticed that the cheerleader isn't there, then they might

know she's not there because of what she did to me. They may not have a

right to, but they would get mad at me. They would retaliate and hurt me,

even though it was all her doing. >>sighs<< I don't know. We'll have to

see what the future holds.

Chapter 5

I began that day like any other. I went to my morning classes, took notes, and appeared to pay attention when the situation warranted it. But my mind was on the upcoming assembly. I couldn't shake the nervous feelings that gripped my body. To compensate for my hands shaking, I tapped my foot. This way, at least my body had an outlet, and nobody could tell how nervous I was. I didn't want to tip anybody off as to why this assembly was taking place. I didn't want anyone to know it was because of me.

After lunch, I went to my 6th period study hall. This is where I usually got most of my morning homework done. That way, I had less work to bring home with me at the end of the day. It may have seemed like a nerdy thing to do, but that wasn't why I did my homework during study hall. I thought that once I left these four walls that I shouldn't have to deal with anything that happened INSIDE of them. That meant homework. The rest of the day was mine, all mine. I could travel to a world that I belonged in, that I was wanted. And nothing was going to interrupt that fact.

"Edwards," the attendant called.

"Here," I softly squeaked back.

Pausing for a minute, the attendant looked up from name call to see that I was actually there.

"And where were you yesterday?" She asked.

"I went home after lunch," I replied.

"Do you have a note with you?"

"No, sorry."

She went back to taking attendance. I was going to have to ask my mother about getting a note excusing me. After all, those were the rules. And I'm not saying that I was a rule-obeyer. I just didn't feel like getting penalized due to my absence. There were exigent circumstances. That's why I left. Didn't she understand that?

The rest of my afternoon classes were torture. All I could focus on was the clock. At 2pm the assembly would begin. The minutes dragged on for hours. Each second that went by, the clock was antagonizing me, purposefully delaying its progression.

Eventually, the clock read 1:55 pm. That's when we all heard the principal announce over the loudspeaker that everyone needed to gather in the gymnasium for the assembly.

The entire school prepared themselves for the upcoming assembly that was being held in the gymnasium. The students climbed onto the bleachers to find a seat while the staff oversaw the commotion, trying to make sure it didn't get too out of hand. As usual, the students filtered through each other to form their own little cliques. Intermittently, there were a few loners. You know the kind I'm talking about. The loners were people who nobody would talk to. Not the jocks, not the cheerleaders, not the geeks or the nerds. So when I say nobody, I mean nobody.

Once everyone had a seat, the principal motioned for everyone to be quiet. I could see a few police officers gathered around him, and a very large chalkboard was just a few feet away from them. My heart began to pound. I had no idea who was going to say what, or what was about to come. I just knew I couldn't wait for it to be over.

"May I have everyone's attention, please?" Mr. Mitchell said into the microphone. Within seconds, the entire gym went into a hushed quiet.

"Thank you," Mr. Mitchell continued. "I bet everyone's wondering why I called this emergency assembly. It has come to my attention that some students are being violent with others. This behavior will not be tolerated, and if I hear of any students hurting other students, they will be arrested. For those of you who have decided that it is acceptable to pick on your fellow classmates, these officers will explain why harassing your classmates is unacceptable." Mr. Mitchell backed away from the podium, and an officer stepped forward.

He was tall, taller than everyone in the room. He must've been 6'4", at least. He had dark hair, which he kept cropped close to his head. He had a stocky build. It reminded me of a giant rectangle. While he was large, he was kind of soft. You know, in the sense that he had a little bit of pudge. I still wouldn't have wanted to be on his bad side.

"Thank you, Mr. Mitchell." The officer began. "My name is Sergeant Lou Saroka with the Fox Grove Police Department. Me and my fellow officers are here to teach you about violence in schools. "

"Most of you may not be aware, but school violence is a trend that is currently on the rise." Sgt. Saroka continued. "The problem with school violence is that very few people understand the dynamics. So this cycle of violence continues. " He walked over to the chalkboard. He drew a large circle with arrows inside of it, suggesting that the circle went around itself. Then he drew a squiggly line that went in one direction. He pointed to the squiggly line.

"This is the line that the academy taught us about Battered Person Syndrome. When one person in a domestic relationship becomes abusive, the other person in the relationship is what we officers call the "battered spouse". Battered spouses suffer from low self esteem, and believe that the abuse is their fault. The battered spouses often tell themselves that it's their fault, and they usually end up rejecting all forms of help offered to them."

"This part of the line," Sgt. Saroka pointed to the part where the squiggle went upwards, "represents the tension building stage. In this stage, there is building abuse suffered by the battered spouse. The abuser may also slap their spouse around, continually demeaning them and abusing them. The abuse is not only physical. The abuse can come in the emotional form, as well as psychological."

"This part of the line," Sgt. Saroka pointed to the part where the squiggle was at a peak, "is called the Acute Battering Stage. We also call it the "blow out". At this point in the abuse cycle, there is a huge fight. There is where typically the police are called in."

"And this part," Sgt Saroka pointed to the downwards slope of the squiggle, "is called the Loving Contribution stage. This stage is characterized by a lot of, 'Oh baby, I'm sorry. I'll never do that again. I promise I'll change. Things will be different from now on.' The abuser may even buy the battered spouse gifts. But if you notice," he pointed to the next upward squiggle, "the cycle of abuse doesn't stop. It keeps going and going until eventually, the battered spouse either leaves the abuser or worse. The battered spouse kills their abuser."

"To a battered spouse, killing their abuser is the only way to make the violence stop. Battered spouses feel that if they leave their abusers, that their lives are still in danger. They feel that their abusers will come after them, stalk them, and never let them escape the violence and control. That's why many of them kill their abusive spouses."

"School violence is similar to Battered Spouse Syndrome because both of the victims feel hopeless. Both of the victims feel that nothing will make this situation better. Nothing will make their abusers happy. However, Battered spouses typically stay with their abusive partners out of love. That is why the cycle goes up and down several times. In schools, the abuse arrives out of the blue. The student on the receiving end of the abuse isn't looking for approval from their peers. The abused student, nine times out of ten, has done nothing to warrant the start of the abuse cycle. So when the abused student feels hopeless and suffers from low self esteem, that when the situation can go from bad to worse. Since the abused student didn't seek out the attention, they feel there is no way to escape it. That's why a lot of instances of school violence go unreported. The abused student often resorts to escalated measures of violence to make the abuser stop. That is when innocent bystanders get hurt. When the abused student escalates the violence, which is when the situation can no longer be diffused."

He paused for a moment, allowing the students to wrap their minds around his words. Looking around, I could see that it had a mixed reaction. Some of the students understood. Some didn't. And some were

very close to understanding, but couldn't quite put the final piece of the

puzzle together.

Taking a deep breath, Sgt Saroka continued. "You kids may be

wondering why an individual chooses to behave this way in the first place.

Let me clarify the abuser's stance for you all. The abuser doesn't wake up

one day and say, 'Gee, I think I'm going to hurt someone today.' Their

behavior is a progressive downward spiral. Typically, abusers act the way

they do for one of three reasons. The first reason is a need. Whatever the

need is, it's not being met. And this angers the abuser. So in turn, the

individual becomes abusive in order to have their needs met. They put

their needs above everything else, including other people's safety. This is

when the abuse cycle can become really volatile. The second reason an

individual may become abusive is control. When these needs aren't being

met, the person will do everything in their power to make their needs

everyone else's number one top priority."

"Sadly to say, the abuser's needs are never met. Hence, that is why

they continue to be abusive. And that is why most of the time, the violence only escalates." A student sitting in the second row raised his hand. Sgt Saroka pointed at him and said, "Yes, son. You have a question?"

"Uh, yeah. You said there were three reasons. What's the third?" He said in a hushed monotone.

"That is a good question. The third one may not be 100% clear to you kids. If anyone doesn't understand, please stop me and ask me about it." Sgt Saroka smiled.

"The third reason that an individual would hurt another individual is power. When an individual says or does something that hurts someone, that individual assumes a dominant role. This dominance comes from the lack of control in their own life, so they lash out at whoever they perceive to be weaker, or submissive.

"Instead of admitting that they feel weak or that they need help with something in their life, they try to overcompensate by acting tough. That weakness in their character becomes an unconscious obsession for them. That is why a lot of people in that position don't ask for help. They may not even know it's there.

"But you can help them," Sgt Saroka continued. "If you see someone picking on someone else, you can notify someone. Tell a teacher. Tell the principal. Tell your parents. Or come talk to us down at the station. But every single one of you has the power to diffuse a potentially dangerous situation."

During the rest of the assembly, Sgt Saroka answered questions from everyone, including the staff. I sat their in silence, letting his words be processed in my memory banks.

To some degree, what he said made sense. But I had this nagging feeling that something was missing. I couldn't quite put my finger on it, but there was a piece of the puzzle that wasn't set down in place. It aggravated me. I had to figure it out!

I didn't even notice when the assembly was over. I just noticed that everyone seemed to be shuffling towards the doors. Grabbing my bag, I stood up and began to glide my feet towards the door. That's when I saw my mom. She was leaning up against the wall with her arms folded across her chest. She was conversing with a teacher I didn't know. Casually, I made my way over.

"Hey, baby." Mom said with a smile. I smiled back.

"Hey mom." What a response!

"What did you think of it?" She asked. Mom and the teacher looked at me, waiting for an answer.

"It was good. What he said made sense." I didn't want to bring up my nagging feeling. Unless I could articulate the exact piece that I felt was missing, I didn't have a valid foundation to stand on.

"Well, would you like to go talk to Sgt Saroka now?" Mom wrapped her arm around my shoulder.

"Sure, I guess."

Striding together side by side, we turned around and walked back over to the police officers and to the majority of the administration staff.

"Good afternoon, Sergeant." My mom sounded slightly chipper as she greeted the announcer.

"Good afternoon, Ma'am." He responded.

"This is the lady I told you about," Mr. Petersen waved his hand at my mother.

Sgt Saroka extended his hand. "Nice to meet you."

"Nice to meet you, too." Mom replied. "This is my daughter, Robin."

Now it was my turn. I extended my hand and exchanged pleasantries.

"That's a nice eye you've got there," Sgt Saroka observed.

"Thanks," I mumbled. I wasn't quite sure what to say to that comment. I stared at the floor.

"What happened?" He took a step towards me, trying to initiate a personal conversation. I didn't understand why adults did that, but it seemed to be a trend of comfort that they possessed and we adolescents did not.

"Well, yesterday I was at my locker during lunch and a cheerleader pushed me inside of it." I replied.

"How do you know it was a cheerleader?"

"Because when I looked around, I saw a group of cheerleaders walking down the hall laughing."

"And how do you know which cheerleader did it?"

"I don't. Not 100%. But the cheerleader whose locker is next to mine is always pushing me and kicking my books down the hallway everyday." Finally, I gazed up. Sgt Saroka and I made eye contact.

"So you just assumed it was her who pushed you."

"Yeah, I guess."

"Well, it was a good guess. She confessed to being the one who pushed you."

"Mom said that the cheerleader was going to be charged," I asked. I don't know what made me say that, but I was glad I did. Maybe I'd get to be in on the information circle. Maybe I could find out what was going on.

"Yes we are," Sgt Saroka said. "What she did was assault on a minor. That's a Class C felony."

"How do you classify it as a Class C felony?" Mom asked.

"A person is guilty of gang assault in the second degree when, with intent to cause physical injury to another person and when aided by two or more other persons actually present, he causes serious physical injury to such person or to a third person." Sgt Saroka replied with an air of confidence.

"I don't understand. They're cheerleaders, not a gang." I said, bewildered.

"The term gang doesn't necessarily mean a gang. It means that there were two or more people compared to your one person. It just means you were severely outnumbered," Sgt Saroka explained.

"Oh," I murmured. I was beginning to understand their line of thinking now. "What's the punishment for a Class C felony?"

"Well, it depends. Usually, a person convicted of a Class C felony will serve seven years in prison. However, this is her first offense. So she might get time off if she behaves herself. Plus, she'll have a felony conviction on her permanent record for the rest of her life." Sgt Saroka sounded like a text book of penal code knowledge.

I nodded, absorbing even more information. "Does that mean there'll be a trial?"

"Most likely. The only way there won't be is if she pleads guilty. If there is a trial, would you be okay testifying as to what happened?" Sgt Saroka delicately placed his hand on my shoulder. I knew the gesture was supposed to be a sign of support, but I was a little intimidated.

"Yeah, I guess. I mean, I don't want her doing this to anyone else. Plus, I never did anything to her. I don't even know her name," I shrugged, trying to look on the bright side. This sucked. It was beginning to sound like things were going to get worse before they got better.

The rest of the "adult" conversation was a blur. I mentally came and went, although I wasn't really sure where I went when I wasn't listening to them and nodding in agreement. I just wandered off.

After more unnecessary time was spent, Mom and I finally decided to head home. When I got there, I immediately went to my computer. I knew that writing in my journal would help me sort out this mess I called a mind.

October 11, 2006 3:12 pm

That assembly wasn't as bad as I thought it would be. It was very

informative. I couldn't shake this feeling that they missed something. I

can't figure it out! It's driving me nuts! Oh well. It'll come to me sooner

or later. I guess that cheerleader is going to be charged with a felony! I

can't believe it! She'll be 24 before she gets out! That's crazy! I kind of

feel bad, almost like it's my fault. But I know it's not. She pushed me. I

didn't do anything to her. And it's not like any of her friends stood up to

her. I wonder if their getting charged. Do you have to charge more than

one person to be able to charge someone with 'gang assault'? Hm. I'll

have to ask Sergeant Saroka about that the next time I see him. He also

said that we might have to go to trial if she doesn't plead guilty. That'll be

so weird to go to trial. What will everyone at school say? Will they stand

behind me? Or will they get mad at me? Technically, they have no reason

to get mad at me. It wasn't my decision to have her push me into my

locker. It wasn't my decision to press charges, and it wasn't my decision

that she gets in this much trouble. I don't know. I just have a bad feeling that a lot of people are going to get pissed at me about this. They better

not! I'm getting sick of this crap! I never do anything to them! Why can't

they leave me alone?!

Chapter 6

I had the worst time trying to sleep that night. I tossed and turned all night. While my body was exhausted and patiently welcomed the escaping world of sleep and dreams, my brain would not turn off. It was a computer on stand by mode. Even though I told it to shut down, it just went idle.

I kept wondering what everyone's reaction was going to be tomorrow. I wondered if this would hamper the violence. I had more questions since the deliverance of the assembly, but I had no idea of how or where to find the answers I sought. What was going to happen to the cheerleader? How was everyone else going to react to the assembly? Would anyone know I had something to do with it? Are they that smart, or are they so wrapped up in their own existence that they will be clueless? What are they going to think of my black eye? Are they even going to notice? If I tell them I tripped, will they believe me? What if they retaliate? Do they like the cheerleader enough to hurt me because she got in trouble for what she did to me? Or do they not care?

I had no way of stopping the torrential tsunami of thoughts from overflowing my conscious mind. It began to give me a tension headache as I listened to the sound of late night/early morning traffic just a quarter mile away on the highway.

Sighing, I decided to stop fighting the thoughts. As they took over the emotional control center of my soul, I tossed and turned until the metallic drill sergeant instructed me to rise and shine.

Alright, fine. I grumbled to myself. *I'll rise, but I refuse to shine.*

Slapping my alarm clock silent, I slowly rolled out of bed. Throwing on the nearest clothes I could find on the floor, I decided to wander downstairs. The front of my mind was plagued with questions, and the core of my soul told me it couldn't hurt to ask the matriarchal advice of the elderly counsel.

Meandering around the house, I followed the invisible chain to the "leader". Ending up in the kitchen, I began my bombardment of endless questions.

"Hey kiddo. What's up?" Mom asked, smiling at me from behind her morning cup of coffee.

"Not much. I was wondering a few things." I said cautiously.

"Like what?" She inquired. She continued to sip her cup of coffee.

"Well, for one thing, I was wondering what happens now? Now that we had the assembly, what do we do?" I began.

"We go to court and deal with that girl who decided its okay to hurt people and tell her that it's not. That's what we do." Mom answered.

"Okay. What are the other kids going to think? Are they going to be mad at me? Are they going to side with her because she's popular? Are they going to hate me? Are they going to retaliate because they're mad that she got in trouble?" The outpouring of questions must've been overbearing first thing in the morning, but the burning questions flowed out faster than I could excogitate them.

"I don't know what the other kids are going to think. I would imagine that they are going to be grateful for what you have done. You're trying to protect everyone from being hurt, from violence. As for people being mad at that girl, they should be mad at her. What she did was a poor decision, and nobody forced her to do what she did. That was entirely her choice. If they don't want to be mad at her, then they should get mad at her parents for raising her to make such poor choices with no forethought to the possible consequences." Mom said confidently. There was a slight edge to her voice, as if the concept of that girl ired my mother. "Why are you asking so many questions?"

"I don't know," I shrugged. "I'm just worried."

"What are you worried about, honey?" She peered at me through a puzzled expression.

I sighed. "I'm not exactly sure. I guess I'm worried that the other kids are going to get mad at me because she got in trouble. And I know that it was the cheerleader's fault she got in trouble. You're right. No one forced her to push me into my locker. But that doesn't mean they won't get mad that she's not at school. And I don't want anymore attacks to happen. It sucked getting hurt in the first place. How am I supposed to know that it won't happen again?" I babbled, pausing only to take a breath. "Is the trouble over? How do I know it's over?"

"Easy, killer. Down girl. First off, you don't know if it's over. That's why you have to wait and see what happens. And besides, if someone else gets upset because that girl got in trouble and they decide to hurt you, then they themselves are going to get in trouble. Do you understand? And it wouldn't be the end of the world." Mom did her best to shush my qualms.

"I guess. So I pretty much have to wait and see what happens." I summed up mom's advice.

"Yes. Sorry to say that's the way these things go." Mom poured more coffee into her nearly empty mug.

"Okay. Thanks Mom." I turned around, heading back to my room.

"Better hurry up kiddo, or else you're going to be late for school." Her voice echoed behind me.

Running upstairs, I knew one place I could vent.

October 12, 2006   7: 16 am

Damn. I couldn't sleep last night. I'm so worried about what's going to

happen because of that stupid twit. I mean, I just want to know what's

going to happen. I just want to be prepared, I guess. It'd be nice to know if

someone else is going to attack me. Maybe I should just start wearing a

helmet. Lol, then I'd be like those retarded football players. Duhhhh,

what's going on? Hahahaha. Thank goodness I'm not stupid like them.

Maybe that's why I'm not one of the popular kids. Because I'm not "non

compos mentus". Well, I got to get ready to suffer another day at Hell

Grove High.

Chapter 7

My nerves were seething with raw anticipation even before I made my way up the pathway towards confronting the anticipation. I had no idea what was to come of the day after the assembly, and I wasn't sure if I wanted to know.

As we pulled up to the cul-de-sac where all the other mother hens dropped off their young chicklets, mom turned to me.

"Before you go, I have something I want to discuss with you." Mom said. For some reason, that got my nerves' attention, making my body resemble an epileptics. Reaching inside her purse, her hand wrapped around something small. She pulled it out, and I could see a slight lavender tinge to a corner that stuck out from the side of her palm. She placed the technological leash in my lap.

"This is in case of an emergency. If anything happens to you at school, you can call me immediately. I have already programmed my number in there. Okay, honey?" Mom's face radiated with compassion and grace as she read my face for a response.

"Okay. Thanks mom." I said, placing it in my own little mini purse. I smiled one last time before exiting the vehicle. Walking up to the entrance, my mind had already wandered off to a far off place.

I couldn't shake the awful feeling of dread that caressed my soul the night before, the monster that deprived me of all of my senses except for the one it invoked. My body responded to its toxic side effects. I felt like a marionette, kept away from making my own voluntary actions. Whenever I pleaded with the demon to let me go, it would riposte the strings quickly, jerking me one way or the other as it pleased.

I waited in homeroom, the class before class begun. All the other cattle took their seats as our attendance was taken. Occasionally, I glanced around.

No one even notices my black eye. It's still as if I don't exist, I thought to myself. While I was bewildered by everyone's lack of attention, I was partially relieved. It was nice to still be invisible. But this was just the beginning. It was only my first class. I had to wait out the rest of the day to find out if anyone was going to notice it. I also had to wait and see if anyone was smart enough to associate the anti-violence assembly with my

black eye and the cheerleader's absence.

Second period went by much the same. Then again, it was gym. My

peers were too concerned with running faster than all of the other hamsters

on their wheels.

Damn, I thought. *I hate dodge ball. Actually, I like dodge ball. I just

don't like getting hit by the ball*s! I snickered to myself. I got a kick out of

semantics, especially when they were "inside" jokes.

Luckily I made it through gym without getting hit more than a dozen

times in the head. I didn't care if the soft plastic design was meant to

relieve some of the impact of the ball hitting flesh. It still hurt.

Upon arrival of Mrs. Grant's class, I was beginning to relax. Nobody

had said one word about my eye, or the assembly, or the cheerleader, or

anything my "what if" monster had been asking me all night. I had

actually forgotten all about my worries, albeit temporarily.

When the bell rang, I skipped out the door. I actually had an uplifting

beat to my step. I felt care free, as if time had loosened the restraints to my

soul. I could soar high, higher, until I was water skiing on the clouds. I had overcome my demons, and I no longer obsessed about what the teachers were going to think about my eye. None of them had even bothered to pay the slightest attention. Maybe it wasn't as big a deal as I thought it was. Maybe nobody cared about the trivial concerns of the individuals. Maybe they only cared about themselves. If that was the case, then I was off the hook. Nobody would pay attention to me!

I had almost completely relaxed in Mrs. Johnson's class. A dense fog of a copasetic mien entranced me, pulling me in, snogging with my inner desires of peace and tranquility. Time seemed to tick by, and each second resembled the same. The seconds passed by analogously with every single one that went by, and they all melded into the background of high school days past.

But then a voice called to me, pulling me out of the fog.

"Robin, didn't you hear the bell ring?" Mrs. Johnson asked. Looking around, I saw that everyone had left. I was the only person sitting there.

"No, I guess I didn't. Sorry." I smiled sheepishly, gathering my things.

Mrs. Johnson sighed. Her dimples began to exercise, pulling her cheeks up to flex their might. "So then where were you?"

Bewildered I asked, "What do you mean, where was I?"

"Well, mentally you weren't here. If you were, you would've heard the bell ring. So what were you thinking about?"

"Well, I was thinking about yesterday." I answered quietly.

"The assembly?"

"Yeah."

"Was there something wrong with the assembly?" Mrs. Johnson asked. I got the feeling that she was trying to be empathetic, but lacked the information necessary to put the puzzle pieces together in their rightful place.

"No," I replied.

"Then what about the assembly?"

I shrugged. I didn't know what to say without sounding narcissistic.

"It's okay, Robin. You can tell me. Did something happen at the assembly?" Mrs. Johnson asked again.

"No, nothing happened at the assembly." I answered.

Scanning me like a check out register, her answer came to her.

"Would the assembly have anything to do with your shiner?"

"Yeah." My voice became hushed, barely above a whisper.

"It's okay, Robin. Mr. Petersen explained everything to us teachers before the assembly. You can talk to me about what's going on inside your head, dear." Mrs. Johnson said softly.

For the first time, I actually felt a twinge of hope in my heart. It felt like I could relax for a second that somebody DID care about where I was coming from. Maybe it was an involuntary moment of weakness on my part. Or maybe I had finally come across an adult (other than my mother) whom I could trust. Either way, I sat down at the desk closest towards her and began to rattle off all of my worries, my insecurities. Everything that was on my mind. Slowly, at first. But then everything came pouring out.

"I don't know. I'm worried I guess. I'm worried that people will be mad at me. Will the other students be mad at me? Will the cheerleading coach? Will the adults be mad at me? I have no idea what's going to happen, and I'm scared not knowing. I didn't ask for this to happen, and I wouldn't ask for anything else to happen as a result of my mom getting upset with her. I mean, I'm upset with the cheerleader too, but I didn't decide to get her in trouble. My mom did. And mom says it was the cheerleader's decision to do what she did. Are the other kids going to see it that way? Or are they going to think that, 'Oh. Well the hurt freshman who couldn't take a joke is the one that got her in trouble.' Although, I don't see how that would be a joke at all. It wasn't very funny. In fact, that's why I was late to your class the other day. That stupid cheerleader kicked my books down the hallway right before 3rd period, and Mrs. Grant wanted to know why. I don't know why I didn't tell her. I should've told her. She told me if I was late one more time, then I'd get my third late slip. That would mean I'd get detention! And for what? Because that stupid twit won't leave me alone?! I never do anything to her? Why does she have to be so mean to me?" I paused to take a breath, my blood lit by the rage of my perceived injustice delivered by the hands of the hierarchy of high school.

"So what is it that you're most worried or upset about?" Mrs. Johnson asked. Her voice was soft and compassionate. Her facial expression showed a caring that I had never seen her wear before. As strange as it was, it almost fit her.

"Well, I guess I'm more worried about somebody getting upset because the cheerleader got in trouble. Even though it was her fault, the other kids might still get mad at me. And I'm upset that I have to deal with this in the first place. I didn't start any trouble. I never even look at her, not even when she's standing at her locker, WHICH is right next to mine." I took in a deep breath, raising my gaze to meet hers. "I guess I just want to know what's going to happen next."

"Well, dear. There is no way to know exactly what's going to happen next. But you're right. Nobody has the right to get mad at you because she got in trouble for what she did. That was her decision. Nobody coerced her. She chose that all on her own. And if anyone does retaliate for her getting in trouble, they're only getting themselves in trouble." Mrs. Johnson leaned in close to me. Winking with a smile on her face, she said, "Besides, if anyone does anything to you, you know you can come talk to me about it."

I smiled back. It was nice to know I had a friend. Or at least, someone who cared about me for some of the right reasons.

I went through the rest of the day feeling more relaxed. My inner demons had lost their grip on the strings to my emotions, and I was able to break free of the paralyzing fear that its spell had cast on me.

Even better, I was able to concentrate on my schoolwork. After all, the whole purpose to go to school was to gain an education. Actually, in my opinion, I believed that adults in the government were clueless. I mean, seriously. Why would a person logically spend 13 years learning the same subjects? I was told it was to be able to apply what I learned to real life, but I had no idea how to do that. Plus, I was also told that the job market wanted "well rounded individuals". But that didn't tell me how school was designed to create a person like that. Oh well. Let the adults do what they think is best. After all, they know every single student, right? They know the strengths and weaknesses, ins and outs of everyone that walked through those front doors. Yeah, right.

October 12, 2006 3:17pm

Wow, do I feel retarded now. I was up all night worrying for nothing! I

talked to Mrs. Johnson, and now I have no idea what I was worrying

about! I guess Mr. Petersen told all of the teachers the situation, so now

they think the cheerleader is to blame, too! That's awesome! I'm so glad

for that. And Mrs. Johnson is a lot cooler than I thought she was. When I

started my freshman year, I thought she was one of those serious teachers

who only cared about grades. Turns out, she does care about the students!

That's such a relief. I wonder if all of the teachers feel that way. Do they

all care about what happened? Is that why they're teaching? It can't be for

the money. The way I hear it, teachers don't get paid a lot. Maybe they

love the topic, not the students. Oh well. I'm thinking about asking her if I

can eat lunch in her room. That way, maybe I can have lunch in peace. I

mean, no more people throwing things into my food, no more people

taking my lunch and taking a bite right in front of me (ew, how gross).

This could be awesome! Plus, if I ever had a problem in her class, I could

run right to her. We could talk about it after class. I could tell her what's going on. No more spit balls in my hair. No more crap from them! It sounds wonderful. I'm going to ask her tomorrow. Although, I still need to wait and see if the other students are going to get mad about what happened to the cheerleader. Like my mom and Mrs. Johnson said, they have no reason to. However, that doesn't mean they won't. People don't always act logically. They act emotionally.

Chapter 8

With a renewed confidence, I felt I was more prepared to face my peers. Instead of standing alone to face the mob of thousands, I had the support of the adults backing me up. This, quite possibly, was a battle that I could win. That was good. The fact that the battlefield was one fought with words and not violence, which was good also. In fact, that was even better. That meant I had a chance for survival, and a chance for victory.

Strolling down the halls, I momentarily forgot of everyone else's perceptions of my "shiner". I walked with my head up, enjoying the support that my simulated bubble provided. I had been set free, free from the "what if?" monster.

Looking around, I noticed the other students. Most of them lingered in the hallways, engaged in trivial conversations. Those who saw me seemed to look through me, as if I were a translucent hologram of a peer.

An autonomic force gently tugged on my cheeks, sending the corners of my mouth slightly upward. I couldn't help but smirk at the ability to be invisible, yet walk amongst them. Oh, the irony!

I strolled boldly through the doorway into homeroom. Taking my seat, I set my bag on my lap and rummaged its contents for my first period's books. I knew exactly where they were, as always. They were the first set of books in the front of my bag. And yet, I still always looked through my entire bag just to make sure. How OCD of me.

Picking my head up with confidence rubbing my shoulders, I waited patiently for the bell. I wanted to "carpe diem," as the Romans would say. For some strange reason, it was almost as if I had forgotten entirely about the disfigurement that I temporarily possessed. It didn't occur to me that when I entered someone's peripheral vision, that there was something amiss about my face. But I didn't care. I had the reassuring thought that the ADULTS were my army, at my beck and call. If I needed to fight in a useless war, then I could count on their ranks for support.

Within the cattle hordes in the hallway, I kept my head up. For the first time, I actually looked ahead of me instead of watching my feet take me to my next class.

Gym. What else could I say, except who the hell thought that running around for 40 minutes was a necessary requirement to education?

Oh well. Might as well make the best of it. After all, once I graduate,
I'll never have to be subjected to gym again. I thought to myself. Waiting
in the gym for the teacher to take attendance, I began to think about the
trial. What would it entail? What kind of questions would be asked?
Would anyone from the school arrive to show support?

"Nice shiner," a voice gently called to me through the mental fog.
Immediately, I snapped back to reality. Looking around, I saw the origin
of the voice.

"Thanks, I think." I smiled, beginning to blush. It was a boy, one I had
never seen before. Looking at him, I'm kind of sorry I hadn't noticed him
before. He was kind of cute. He was half a foot or so taller than me, and
less wiry. His hair contained loose brown curls that he didn't keep too
long, and when the light hit it just right, you could see a reddish glow.
Despite the curls hanging into his eyes, I was able to see the viridity of his
eyes. He had a healthy tan color to his skin, and carried himself
gracefully.

"You're a freshman, right?" He asked with a smile.

"Yeah. What about you?" I smiled back.

"I'm a junior."

"My name's Robin."

"My name's Justin."

"Nice to meet you, Justin."

"Nice to meet you too, Robin. And might I say, you have the perfect little dimples when you smile. I don't know if anyone's ever told you that." He smiled.

I blushed. "No, no one's ever mentioned that."

"I'm surprised. They're in the perfect spot in your smile."

"Well, thank you."

"So how did that happen?" His voice was always a soft gentle whisper. It reminded me of a leaf in autumn floating down through the air.

"I guess I was born with them." I shrugged.

"No, I meant what happened to your eye." He laughed.

"Oh." I started laughing. "I'm sorry. God, I'm such a dork."

"Hey, there's nothing wrong with dorks. Dorks are cool." We continued laughing until the teen awkwardness had slightly subsided.

"Some girl pushed me into my locker."

"What? Like she stuffed you in it?"

"No. I was getting my afternoon books out and she pushed me into it. My eye hit the inside part of the door."

Bewilderment crossed his face. No matter how he contorted it, it looked cute.

"Wow, what a bitch!"

"Yeah, no kidding."

"So what did you do to her?"

"I didn't do anything. I never did. I don't even know her name!"

"Wow, that's messed up." He shook his head. The curls responded, flowing with each shake.

"Yeah, it is."

"O'Reilly! Your participation would be greatly appreciated!" Mrs. Dewitt called from across the room. Justin's head turned to face her, and then looked back at me.

"I got to go." A sheepish smile crossed his face, and I waved as he jogged over to her.

The rest of gym class was hard. I was expected to participate in dodge

ball, but I couldn't keep my attention away from my new acquaintance.

My mind kept replaying the conversation we had, and drifting over to the

land of possibilities. I wondered what he was doing in his side of the gym

with Mrs. Dewitt, and would I ever see him again.

Sighing, I managed to wrangle my attention away from Justin and

focus on the rest of my day. While it was difficult and it made the day

almost unbearably long, I was able to do it.

At the end of the day, I gathered my books out of my locker and

slipped out the side door. I headed down the hill, in the direction of my

house.

I know, I know. Most kids would take the bus rather than walk 20

minutes uphill. However, I wasn't most kids. I was terrified of busses.

Mind you, it wasn't always like that. But something happened in

elementary school that would make me afraid.

One day in the winter of third grade, I boarded the bus with the

expectation of driving the same route to pick up the same nasty children and then be transported to the same elementary school, where I would learn the same material over and over again. It was a monotonous ritual, but it was dependable. I was only 8, but I would learn one of life's most important lessons that day. The lesson being that while routine is nice, life is ultimately unpredictable. And whatever is going to happen will happen, whether or not that's what a person wants.

We were going down a steep hill rather slowly, trying to compensate for the wintry conditions. Once we had arrived at the left turn we were supposed to make, I could feel the bus slowly creep in that direction. Out of nowhere, the bus continued to travel down the road in the position of the left turn. I could hear the driver start to shout as the bus lurched down the hill sideways. The weight of the metal device caused the bus to tip on two wheels, and a bunch of us children screamed. We continued screaming as the bus picked up speed. Shutting my eyes, I curled up in the seat and hoped that we wouldn't tip over.

The whole ordeal only lasted two or three minutes, but it was enough to cause a panic attack anytime I walked near a school bus. The thought of going on one ever again was incomprehensible to me.

Slowly, I walked sideways down the hill. I hated running down it, so I crab-walked. It was the most direct route, and I wasn't unlike the rest of my peers in experiencing the desire to get home ASAP. Once I had hit the highway I tuned out reality, checking in long enough to make sure I could cross the intersection without getting hit.

Coming across the first intersection, I stopped and looked around. Making sure no traffic was coming towards me, I scurried across as fast as possible. Once I had made it across, I slowed my pace down to a walk. As habit took over, I watched my feet alternate in taking the lead, performing a slow yet repetitive waltz with each other.

After a couple of more intersections, I was walking up the street that I called home. I could feel the peace of my sanctum sanctorum tug at my soul, and a sudden burst of energy threw me closer to my destination. Upon arrival, I smiled at my castle. I was home!

Lying down in bed was one of my guiltiest pleasures. For some women, it was chocolate. For some men, it was sex or alcohol. For me, it was bed. The idea that I could take a mini vacation and travel anywhere I wanted to with one unconscious trip was a trip in itself.

I began to recall the day, and kept finding myself thinking of my newly acquired acquaintance. A smile crept over my dimples, revealing their hiding spot. *He's kind of cute,* I smiled to myself. *And sweet.*

Suddenly, a feeling of dread gripped my soul, shaking me to the core. It resembled the brief moments before déjà vu, when you know something cosmic is trying to get your attention. Mulling it over, I tried to figure out why I had a bad feeling when it came to Justin. I didn't know him well enough to put myself in serious peril.

Then it hit me like a flash of lightning across the sky of epiphanies.

Two years ago, during the winter dance in 7th grade, I was dancing in the corner of the gym with myself. While I wasn't bothering anyone, it was a tad depressing to watch dozens of couples paired off. Summoning up the courage, I found a male loner who was sitting on the bleachers.

"What have I got to lose?" I asked myself.

"Would you like to dance with me?" I asked him, putting on a smile.

"Maybe later," he responded. His reaction was indifferent, so I walked away.

It hadn't occurred to me that as time rolled on, he hadn't approached me for that dance I had asked about. That is, not until the dance was over. When I was walking towards the door, I spotted him walking with a male friend.

"Now I'll dance with you," he said. He barely got out the words before him and his friends were cracking up hysterically, at my expense.

While Justin wasn't the guy that was rude, my subconscious was telling me that I shouldn't trust anyone, especially not of the opposite sex.

"Look at your mother," it whispered to me. "She knew that men weren't to be trusted. That's why she divorced your father."

Pushing myself off of my bed, I lurched towards my computer.

October 13, 2006   3:43 pm

I'm very confused right now. I met this guy in my gym class. His name is

Justin. He seems cool, but for some reason, I have a bad feeling about him.

Maybe it's because I've never had any friends. Who knows? All I know is

that I don't like being completely alone, but every time I interact with

another person, I get hurt. Oh well. I'll figure it out later. On the bright

side, Justin commented on my eye. He said it wasn't fair what that

cheerleader did to me. It's nice to know that some of the other students are

on my side, too. It's one thing when the adults say something is bad, but

it's another thing when your peers agree with you. Maybe the other

students won't get mad at me when the cheerleader gets in trouble. That'd

be awesome!

Chapter 9

Walking down the stairs, I was greeted with an array of aromas wafting from the kitchen. Immediately, my stomach growled with anticipation.

"Marco," I called out. I never called out "mom" anymore. Not even when we were separated in department stores. Too many other women would always turn their heads and look. They may have known that I wasn't their child and that my voice was strange to them, but it was a habit. They too were called mom, and it was habitual for them to respond. So we decided to say, "Marco polo". This way, we would be unique in our search for each other.

"Polo," my mom's voice replied. She was in the kitchen, responsible for the delicious delectables that were being concocted by her hands.

"Whatcha cooking?" I asked, walking into the room.

"I'm not sure. Right now, I'm just throwing a bunch of things together in a crock pot." Mom responded.

"Ohhhh." I replied, snatching a piece of carrot to nibble on.

"Do you mind?" Mom playfully smacked my hand away from the veggies.

"Nope, don't mind at all." I reached for another one, laughing.

"You are incorrigible!" Mom laughed, continuing to cut vegetables.

"So, how was work?" I asked. My mother was an accountant. It may have seemed boring to the outside world, but she loved her job.

"It was okay. I figured out how to link several spreadsheets together."

Blankly, I looked at my mom. "What spreadsheets?"

"Well, I use different spreadsheets for different companies. I have one spreadsheet for incoming money, one spreadsheet for outgoing money, and the third one is a comparison of the first two. I figured out a formula to type in the top of the spreadsheet that lets me do one change to all three pages instead of having to type the change in three different times."

"Wow, that's impressive. Congrats, mom. I'm proud of you. I wish I was that smart." I smiled at her.

"You are. You may not be as good at accounting as I am, but you have your strengths. Everyone is different, honey. Besides, you wouldn't want everyone to be exactly the same. Then think how monotonous the world would be." She smiled back.

"I know, mom. It's just hard because I'm in school and I have to focus on getting good grades. So I don't really have time to figure out what I'm good at."

"It sounds like you're putting too much emphasis on the wrong things, dear."

"How so?"

"Well, school isn't everything. School is only the beginning. It's designed to give everyone a fair chance at life."

"Well, it's stupid and I hate it."

"Most people aren't crazy about school. But you know what? The really successful people see things that most people don't in school."

"Like what?"

"Well, the people who get far in life see that you can take any little thing that you learn in any of your classes and make a career out of it."

"I don't get it." I shook my head.

"Well, take me for example. I couldn't pass calculus because I would do all of the math in my head and my teacher wanted me to write it down. My teacher wanted to see how I got the answer. However, that doesn't mean I'm bad at math. It just means I do it differently. And because I can whiz through it in my head, I can do accounting."

"Okay…" I said, waiting for the rest of her tangent.

"Well, you have an amazing attention to detail, and an impressive memory. Maybe you can be a scientist. And who knows? Maybe you can find a cure for cancer. You could also be a politician. With your memory and your organizational skills, it's possible."

"Okay…."

"My point is that school is supposed to teach you how to use the skills you have and make the most out of them. Nobody at your school may tell you that, but that's why you go." Mom stopped cutting vegetables and looked me in my face.

"Okay, but that doesn't tell me what I'm supposed to do." My shoulders sagged.

"Nobody is supposed to tell you what to do with your life. You are supposed to figure out what you like to do, what you want to do. And since you're very smart and good at a lot of different things, you have a lot of options as to what you can do for the rest of your life." She smiled at me, and my heart warmed. My mother's advice made sense, more sense than anything anyone else had ever told me. I couldn't help but wonder why people in the school systems didn't tell the children this reason. Maybe more kids would be passionate when it came to their academics.

"So I'm supposed to figure out what I'm going to do career-wise for the rest of my life based on what I like and what I'm good at." I said, summing up her speech.

"Exactly." She resumed her veggie cutting.

"Hmmmm, this is a tough one."

"You don't have to answer right now, dear. You have to have an answer by your senior year. That way, you know what classes to take in college."

"Ahhh. Okay. Thanks mom. So did you do anything else today?"

"Nope. I worked then came home. How about you? How was your day?"

"It wasn't too bad. I met this guy in gym class. He seems nice."

"So I guess we have to have that talk now."

"What talk?" I asked. My heart started pounding, and I could feel the blood pouring into my cheeks. I hoped she wasn't referring to the sex talk.

"The sex talk." Mom looked at me sternly. I wanted to scream and jump out of my skin.

"No, mom. Geez, that's not what I meant." I said, exasperated.

"Are you sure?"

"Yes, I'm sure mom."

"Okay, but now we're going to have that talk soon."

"Whatever, mom."

"Then what did you mean, dear?"

"Well, his name is Justin, and he asked me about my eye. I told him another student did it. He seemed nice. He said it wasn't cool what that cheerleader did." I smiled.

"No honey, it wasn't cool."

"I know mom, but it was different when he said it."

"Oh yeah? And why is that?"

"Because."

"Because why?"

"Because mom."

"Well, I'm trying to understand from your perspective. Can you explain it to me?"

"Okay. Well, it's one thing when an adult says something. Most of the time, kids and grown ups don't agree on things. But this time, the other kids DO agree with me. That's a good thing, especially because it was a kid that did this to me. I don't know. I guess it's nice to know that I'm not totally wrong for thinking she's a bitch."

"Watch your mouth. You're much too pretty to be using ugly language like that. And I see what you mean." Mom added another batch of cut veggies to the pot. I rolled my eyes at her.

"So what are you making for dinner mom? Or are you still undecided?"

"Well, I thought I'd make beef stew."

"Really?" I said, perking up. I loved beef stew.

"Sure. But it won't be ready until tomorrow."

"Oh that's great. That doesn't help us now." I grinned at her.

"I know. So let's think of something to eat together. What are you in the mood for?"

Shrugging, I said, "I don't know. I don't know what we have here."

"So then let's go out and get something."

"Okay, like what?"

"Let's go get a pizza."

"Okay."

"What do you want on it?"

"The usual." I said. Mom starting laughing.

"Don't you want to try something other than green peppers and mushrooms?"

"Nope."

"Oh, come on."

"Why mess with a good thing?"

"Alright, fine." Mom sighed, shaking her head with a smile on her face.

October 13, 2006   8:43 pm

So Mom and I had pizza for dinner. It was delicious, as usual. I told her

about Justin. At first, she thought I had a crush on him. She asked if she

had to give me "the talk". That was so gross. I wish she wouldn't do that.

I'm not stupid. I know how sex works. I took biology. But she said she's

going to give me "the talk" soon. So that gives me a little bit of time to try

and think of a way out of hearing that speech. I know she means well. But

it's still gross. Anyways, mom made beef stew. It'll be ready tomorrow.

I'm so excited. I love beef stew. I could eat the whole pot. But mom

expects me to wait until it's completely cooked. That way, I don't get sick

from eating raw meat. Well, I'm going to go to bed.

Chapter 10

Sitting in homeroom wasn't anything out of the ordinary. I waited the
12 minutes I usually waited for the other students to meander in and find
their seats. The homeroom teacher took her usual attendance and handed
out the usual detention and late slips.

However, this wasn't any usual day. While today may have started out
in the usual manner, it soon became apparent that things had a slight twist.

The homeroom teacher dropped a "see me" slip from the principal's
office on my desk. Incredulously, I stared at the blue piece of paper on my
desk. I had never received one of these. To me, only students like the
cheerleader received these. Good girls like me never got in trouble.

I walked down the halls in a daze towards the main office. I was
vaguely aware of the blur of peers that floated past me, off to complete
their usual routines. I handed the secretary my blue slip, and took a seat
near the principal's office. My body began its own melody, starting with
my pounding heart as the bass. Next was my right foot tapping,

mimicking percussion. The fiery tempo came with the uncertainty as to how the meeting with the principal was going to go.

"Robin Edwards," a male voice called out from the principal's office. Nervously, I stood up and walked towards the door that awaited my future.

"Good morning, Robin." Mr. Mitchell said from his desk. His gaze was focused on some papers on his desk.

"Good morning, Mr. Mitchell." I replied quietly.

"Have a seat." He motioned towards one of the two chairs sitting in front of his desk. You could tell by looking at his office that he took a lot of pride in his job. There wasn't a single unfiled paper to be seen. There was no clutter to speak of. Oddly enough, there were no photographs of loved ones. This was business, and his office showed his seriousness and dedication.

"So, it appears that you missed all of your afternoon classes the other day. And your 6th period teacher said you didn't have a note. Is that correct?" For the first time, Mr. Mitchell's eyes rested on my face. His breathing was even tempered, his body language said business. Nothing about him suggested that he was nervous.

"Yes, sir." I squeaked. My whole body trembled at the prospect of trouble. Air retrieval was a labored task. I was so nervous, and nothing I could've done would've hidden that fact.

"So you admit you skipped all of your afternoon classes?" His monotone voice stated.

"Yes sir." I blinked.

"If you weren't in your classes, where were you?" His questioned seemed innocent, but his tone suggested something sinister. Almost as if I were one of the usual delinquents his path crossed.

"I went home." I answered simply.

"Attendance doesn't have any record of your parents picking you up." He looked through the papers he had in his hand.

"I walked."

"What prompted you to walk home?" Inquisitively, he gazed at me.

I paused, not knowing what to say.

"Well, whatever you reason was, it was the wrong thing to do. I'm going to have to give you detention. I can see in your file that you've been a good girl in the past. Since this is the first time I've had to issue you detention, I'm going to go easy and give you 2 days of lunch detention. Your first day starts Monday." He closed my file, staring at me.

I stared back. On the interstate of nerve synapses there must have been an accident somewhere between my brain and my mouth, because words eluded me.

"You may be excused." Mr. Mitchell stood up, walking to the door. Opening it, he indicated he wanted me to leave so he could continue conducting unnecessary torture on his adopted children.

Numbly, I walked out of his office and to my first period class. I couldn't translate the events that had transpired into tangible reality. It was almost as if I had been having a bad nightmare, and yet, I had been awake through the whole thing.

Dryly, I snickered. A thought occurred to me: Thank goodness It's Friday.

October 14, 2006 3:42 pm

Today just plain sucked. There are no other words to describe it. I got

lunch detention for the first time ever today! That's bullshit! I'm so pissed

off about it. I want to smack someone! I don't get it. That bitch can sit

there and push me into a locker, and I get in trouble? What the hell is that

about? The principal said it was because I missed my afternoon classes.

Well, duh. My eye was killing me, and there was nobody in the nurses'

office. I'm really going to go to the main office to get a damn ice pack.

Morons. They're all so stupid. If I wanted to talk to someone about what

had happened, I would have. But I wanted my eye to stop hurting. Talking

to someone about what had happened wouldn't have made my eye stop

hurting. There's no way out of detention. I wish there was. I don't want to

deal with it. If I skip though, I'll get more detention. I might as well suck

it up and get it over with. What I don't understand is why. If I don't bother

anyone, why do people have to bother me? Why can't they just leave me

alone?

Chapter 11

The entire weekend, I couldn't focus on anything except the impending

torture that would commence next week. Was it really necessary? I asked

myself. I shook my head, partly out of disagreement and partly out of

disbelief. Physically, I wandered from class to class. Mentally, I had

checked out even before I had left Mr. Mitchell's office.

At the end of the day, I threw my entire bag into my locker and slipped

out the door. There was absolutely no way I planned on engaging in

anything related to high school during my weekend. As the minutes had

expired through my day, the waves of shock ebbed its way out as the high

tides of anger alternated its cycle of control. I knew the walk home

wouldn't calm me down. I was mad and getting madder by each passing

second.

I had never been this angry over something so trivial that was out of

my control. I couldn't shake it. Even once I had reached home, all I could

do was pace in every single room I went into. I was losing touch with all of my senses. I hadn't even realized that I was no longer alone, and that my only confidant had graced me with her presence.

"Hi, honey. What's up?" Mom asked with a giant smile.

"Nothing." I spat back.

"Aww, what's wrong?" Mom cooed. Her good mood was strong, unwavering. That was a good thing, because I didn't want my bad mood to put her in a bad mood.

"I have lunch detention next week." I grumbled. I could've been told I won a million dollars, and I would still have replied grouchily.

"Why?" Mom's puzzled expression temporarily concealed her delight at the prospective upcoming weekend.

"'Because I missed my afternoon classes, and my study hall teacher said I didn't have a note.'" I misquoted the principal.

"Well honey, those are school rules." She said soothingly, trying to calm me down.

I just shook my head. I knew those were the rules, but I didn't care.

"So why don't you have a seat, and I'll make us each a cup of tea and we can talk about it. How does that sound?" Walking over to the cabinets, mom pulled out two mugs.

"Whatever." I shrugged, taking a seat at the table.

"Start with what happened in Mr. Mitchell's office. Tell me everything." She glided across the kitchen tiles over to the teapot, where the sound of modern technology made its presence known. It was an unmistakable and familiar sound, the sound of running water.

"Well, I was in homeroom minding my own business when the homeroom teacher gave me a slip saying the principal wanted to see me. So I went down there and he started talking to me about the day that I went home." I spat.

"Why did that upset you so much?" Mom asked, the words delicately rolling through the valley of her vocal chords into the open air.

"It pissed me off because of why I left."

"That was the day that the cheerleader pushed you into the locker, right?" Turning on the stove, she set the teapot on direct heat.

"Yeah."

"Okay, so why did you leave? Why didn't you go to the main office?"

"He asked me the same question." It wasn't an answer, but it was the first answer that came to my mouth.

"And what did you tell him?" Mom sat down next to me. She had nothing to do but wait for the water to boil and listen to my tangent.

"I don't know. I guess I didn't tell him anything." I shrugged. The realization of me myself not knowing why I didn't temporarily distracted me from my anger.

"Why do you think you didn't go to the main office for help?" She rested her head in her hands, staring and smiling at me with her mom-like compassion and sympathy.

"I don't know. I guess it's because I got hurt. That's why I went to the nurses' office. I mean, yeah, it was a problem, but I couldn't have gotten an ice pack at the main office." My response was ever so slightly dripping with sarcasm as the obviousness of the logic of my statement was apparent, if only apparent to me.

"But the cheerleader pushing you into a locker <u>was</u> a problem. That's why you should've gone to the main office. You needed help with getting her to leave you alone."

I just shook my head again for the unknownth time that day. "I know it was a problem, mom. But tattling on her isn't going to make anything better. It wasn't going to make my eye stop hurting. The damage was done. Even if that particular cheerleader leaves me alone the rest of my life, knowing my luck, someone else will start giving me crap. Probably one of her friends. And it would be worse if they did it, especially if I tattled on her."

"That may be so, but you have to learn to stand up for yourself. If someone is harassing you honey, you have the right to a safe and productive education." Mom smiled, rubbing my shoulder. The teapot began to whistle at the affectionate display, prompting her to attend immediately to its beck and call.

"I have no problem standing up for myself, mom. What I'm saying is that it wouldn't matter if I said something. Someone will always be giving me crap. I'll never just be left alone. I mean, it's not like I give them crap, but for some reason, they have to give it to me." My anger was slightly

subsiding throughout the discussion, but bitterness and resentment

lingered.

"Well, there has to be some way that we can make this situation better.

After all, you have 3 ½ more years of high school. You can't just quit

because it's hard." Mom repeatedly dipped her tea bag in her mug.

"I never said I was going to quit school, mom." I looked up at her as

she placed a mug in front of me.

"That's good." She said absent mindedly, still dipping her tea bag.

I just sighed. It felt like this conversation wasn't going anywhere.

Whether the wrong words were being said or the right words weren't, I

wasn't about to stick around and find out.

"I'm going upstairs." Standing up from the table, I quickly escaped the

current situation into complete solitude.

"No, you're not. Come sit down here and finish discussing this with

me." Mom looked up from her tea, giving me a look that there was no

negotiating.

Sighing, I slumped back into my chair with a heavy thud. Waving my right hand at her, I signaled her to talk.

"So you're upset about having lunch detention because you missed the rest of your afternoon classes." Mom began.

"Yeah."

"And you're upset that the principal said you should've gone to the main office since no one was in the nurses' office." She continued.

"Yeah."

"And you disagree with his logic."

"Yes." I said through clenched teeth.

"Why?" She asked, sipping her tea.

"I already told you. I was injured. That's why I went to the nurses' office. I went for an ice pack to put over my eye. If the main office had ice packs, then I would've gone there. But they don't. They would've sent me to the nurses' office. So why bother wasting my time going to the main office at all when they would've sent me where I went in the first place?" I snapped.

"Maybe Mr. Mitchell thought you should've told them there was a problem."

"What the hell good would that have done?"

"Watch your mouth, young lady. I know you're upset and frustrated, but language like that isn't going to fix anything. You're smart enough to think of the appropriate words to get your message across."

"Sorry." My shoulders sagged forward. I was feeling defeated, like nothing I could've said or done was going to make a difference in this conversation.

That was never a good thing. When I felt like I wasn't being heard, I had a tendency to shut down. I didn't communicate, and I didn't listen. What was the point? And when that happened, nothing got accomplished.

"So why didn't you go see Mr. Mitchell?" Mom pushed the subject.

"I don't know." I replied, looking at my cup of tea.

"Well, there must've been a reason."

"I don't know." I reiterated. I was non-compliant, and headed towards belligerent.

"Well, think about it." Mom urged.

I glared at her. If looks could kill, she would've been torn into millions of miniscule particles with all of the icy daggers my eyes could have projected.

"Well?" Her impatience was beginning to filter into her voice.

"Well what? I needed a damn ice pack, so I went to the nurses' office! I didn't go to the principal's office because I wasn't in trouble! There was no point in me going to the principal's office! That would've resulted in more crap from that bitch! I didn't want more crap! I wanted a damn ice pack!" I exploded, slamming my hands on the table.

"Watch your mouth!" Mom yelled back.

"No! Fuck this! I'm going upstairs!" I ran out of the room, bounding towards a safe haven.

"This conversation isn't over!" She yelled after me.

"The hell it isn't!" I yelled back over my shoulder.

October 16, 2006 6:42pm

Omg that was complete and utter bullshit! Mom wanted to have a talk

about me getting detention. She agrees with the principal for giving me

detention. She kept bugging me about not going to Mr. Mitchell's office

for help. If telling the principal what that bitch did would've helped, I

would have. But it would've made things worse. Her and her friends

would've gotten pissed off at me for getting them into trouble, and they

would've attacked me even more. Why don't adults understand that? And

they say kids aren't smart enough. That's bullshit! We're plenty smart

enough. It's just that adults don't understand us. Just because they know

something, doesn't mean they understand it. All I'm trying to do is get

through school so I can get away from this. I'm not trying to create more

drama. I'm just trying to survive. Is that so hard to understand?

Chapter 12

That Monday morning, I was a nervous wreck. I hadn't been able to enjoy my weekend at all, not with detention looming over the horizon. I couldn't even enjoy the thought of gym class, and being able to see Justin.

His perfect curls bounced up and down as he strode over towards me. Giving a half hearted smile, I waved at him.

"Hey," Justin said with a smile.

"Hey." I responded with less enthusiasm.

"Aw, what's wrong?" He said, exaggerating a pout at me.

"I have lunch detention today and tomorrow." I scowled. The thought of detention still irritated me, like sand paper on porcelain.

"For what?" Bewilderment crossed his face. It was still cute.

"Because I went home instead of to the principal's office."

"When?"

"When that stupid bitch pushed me into my locker."

"Why didn't you go to the nurses' office?" He asked softly.

"I did, but nobody was there! I went to the nurses' office for an ice

pack. I would've gone to the principal's office, but they would've sent me

to the nurses' office! I didn't want to complain about what happened and

get her in trouble. All I wanted was an ice pack! That's why I walked

home. So I could get an ice pack!" I said, slightly exasperated.

"So they gave you lunch detention? That's bogus!" Justin's

sympathetic tone was a soothing melody to my heart. It was nice to have

somebody understand what I was saying.

"Yeah, but what can I do? If I skip, they'll give me more lunch

detention or worse, in school suspension. And Mr. Mitchell won't listen to

me when I tell him I just wanted an ice pack." I shrugged, feeling slightly

defeated.

"So go and get the lunch detention over with." Justin smiled at me.

"Yeah." I said sadly.

"Oh, it's not that bad. I've done it plenty of times. If you want, I could

go with you." He offered his companionship with a smile and a hand.

Confused, I looked back and forth between his hand and his face. Why would you offer to go to detention if you didn't have to? But his eyes were so soft, that an unseen force prompted me to reach out.....

"I'd like that." I smiled, taking his hand. It felt warm and soft around my own. He smiled back.

"Awesome. What period do you have lunch?" His velvety voice floated atop his smile, and his spirit wrapped its happiness around me.

"Fifth." I replied, still smiling.

"O'Reilly." Mrs. Dewitt called Justin's name.

"Here!" He yelled in her direction. "I got to go. I'll meet you outside the detention room right before 5th period." He said, letting go of my hand.

"But I don't know where it is!" I called after him. Panic slowly crept up inside of me, threatening to disrupt a newly acquired happy moment.

"It's right across the hall from the gym." Justin called back. While I couldn't see his face, I could picture his smile. I smiled back.

****

Although the bell signaling the end of 4th period had rang less than a minute ago, you wouldn't have known. There was virtually no one in sight. Everyone had already crossed the bridge that contained brighter pastures of meals uneaten.

Not me. I wouldn't be crossing the threshold of lunch heaven. I had detention. Leaning up against the side of the door, I sighed. Clutching my bag, I looked up and down the halls for Justin. No sign. I knew in the back of my mind that whether or not he kept his word, I had to enter the tomb that replaced my pabulum.

"Hey!" Justin's voice ran down the hallway, greeting me with the announcement of his arrival. He was jogging towards me.

"Hey yourself," I replied, relieved that I had a companion. The bell screamed over the loudspeaker, indicating we were late. I gave him a look that told him I was afraid to be late, and I didn't want more detention because I was late.

"Relax, it'll be fine." Extending his arm, Justin opened the door for me. I nodded a slight thanks and walked inside with my escort right behind me.

There was a short man sitting at a desk. He was reading names from a list (I assume he was taking attendance) when he saw us enter.

"Mr. O'Reilly. Welcome back." He said dryly.

"Sup, Mr. Fout?" Justin grinned. He seemed to take pleasure in the irritation that his presence caused the supervisor.

"And who is your friend?" Mr. Fout asked.

"This is Robin. She has detention today, and I offered to escort her." Justin walked over to two available desks and flopped down. I remained steadfast by the door, glued to my tracks.

"Does Robin have a last name?"

"Edwards." I spoke quietly. I didn't move. I didn't blink. It resembled a scene involving a wild animal. If the prey was real still, maybe the predator would pass it.

"Louder." Mr. Fout kept the same monotone voice.

"Edwards." I half shouted, half spoke.

"Ahh, there you are. Have a seat." He smiled, putting a check mark on his paper. He didn't seem to notice my fear driven paralysis. Very slowly, I complied with his order. Justin grinned at me the whole time I inched over to him and slid down in the seat next to him, trying to hide. Looking

around, I absorbed my surroundings. The floors were a dingy white tile.

There were three windows in the entire room. They weren't normal

windows; they were designed much smaller than the other windows in the

school. The desks were arranged to be pushed against the walls, facing

them. Whoever designed the room did their best to inhibit anyone from

speaking to each other. The walls were a prison grayish-white with only

one poster to decorate it. The one poster was a list of rules. "How festive,"

I thought dryly. Looking to Justin for guidance, he smirked at me. I don't

know what he found amusing about this jerry-rigged prison. I pulled the

corner of my cheeks up, but my eyes revealed the truth about the lack of

enthusiasm in my smile.

"For those of you who are new to detention, I will go over the rules

with you," Mr. Fout began. "There is no talking. If you need help, raise

your hand and I will help you. At :15 after, you can put in an order for

lunch. At :25 after, it will be delivered to the room. At 40 after, you're all

excused. If you're new, it is advisable to bring something to do here. If

you have to go to the bathroom, there is one in the back right corner of the room. Under no circumstances are you allowed to leave your desk without

permission. You must raise your hand and ask before doing anything. Any

questions?" Mr. Fout asked in the same monotone voice. Standing up, he

walked over to the door, closed it, and returned to his seat. "Good," and

with that last word, he returned his attention to a crossword puzzle on his

desk.

Glancing up at the clock, it read 11:04 am. I groaned inwardly. Only 4

minutes had passed. There was 36 minutes of tortured imprisonment left. I

could feel my stomach growl in protest at the deprivation of its manna. My

heart broke a little with the powerlessness that I felt at not being able to

feed my body and soul, at the thought of being caged like an animal that

had piddled on the rug. The hole inside of me grew like a black hole at the

realization that my personal break had been stolen from me. I loved lunch.

Not just because I got to eat (and by the time I had been up for 5 hours I

was hungry), but because it gave me a chance to escape. When the bell

rang for lunch, it was as if the plangent sounds of the nasty insults hurled

by my peers faded off into the background. They became hazy, fuzzy, and

almost unrecognizable as something so innocent and pure glowed with its own importance. During lunch, food took all of my attention off of the harsh realities of school. Food was never mean or cruel. It just was. In fact, you could say that food was the only true friend I had in high school.

In a futile attempt to distract myself, I took out my assignment book. Rather than allow the seconds to drag by, I decided to entertain the thought of doing homework. "Let's see," My angelic inner voice whispered to me. "There's an outline for an essay in English I could do. Or I could answer the six questions that are due tomorrow for biology." Its soothing voice offered no comfort. However, I decided on the outline. It would be easy enough to do. We've done dozens in English before, and it had become almost mindless work.

Writing my name at the top of the paper, I paused. Normally, I didn't require my heart to be in the assignment I was working on. But for some reason, it was as if every fiber of my soul protested at the thought of doing homework. Was it because I usually completed my homework during study hall, and this was out of my normal routine? Or was it simply my subconscious way of rebelling against detention? While I was unsure of the specifics, I knew it would be next to impossible to get any work done.

Putting my pencil down, I sighed. Glancing up at the clock, it told me only two minutes had passed since the last time I inquired.

My mind blissfully ran to lunches I had previously eaten, recalling the sights, smells, and all of the wondrous minutes I had spent in the cafeteria. During 5th period, I would always cursorily switch my morning books with my afternoon books. Every second was precious. The faster I got to the line in the cafeteria for food, the less time I had to wait. Once I had arrived within 2 yards of the door the smells eagerly greeted me, and my stomach always replied the greeting. The options the lunch ladies bestowed upon me left me nonplussed. It was always the highlight of my day to solve the mystery of what manna I was going to enjoy. My favorite option of all time was mashed potatoes covered with chicken gravy. It was delicious! There were other options that I enjoyed almost as much (although, nothing could compare with my all time favorite). I liked chicken nuggets and tater tots, spaghetti and meatballs (even though I would always push the meatballs to the side), chips, sodas, anything! The cafeteria was a new world to discover every single day. The discovery process made my heart soar, and almost made up for the torment I endured in the morning just to reach that sacred room.

When those wonderful women had bequeathed my lunch unto me, I gratefully accepted, turning to march my usual path to the corner of the room, right next to those wonderful ladies' entry door.

All of the other peers would sit at the tables. Not me. I would sit in the corner of the room, on the floor, out of everybody's way. This way, there were no territory wars as to who would sit at what table and "omg! We can't sit at that table because SHE'S sitting there" crap. All morning, I had dealt with name calling and stares and snickers and things being thrown at me. But at lunch time, they were (almost) all too busy to torment me, abuse me, ridicule and harass me. They too were hungry. They too were diving into their own manna. They chose to grant me a reprieve for 40 wonderful minutes.

A reprieve that was currently being denied to me, that I couldn't embrace. Instead, I was trapped inside this prison. While this makeshift dungeon was only temporary, it was still replacing my beloved reprieve and denying my manna.

"Whatcha doing'?" Justin leaned in and whispered, distracting me from my thoughts.

"I'm trying to do English." I replied. The lack of enthusiasm in my answer gave away my irritation and resentment towards detention. "Key word being 'trying'."

"Yeah, sometimes it's hard to do homework in here." Justin nodded sympathetically. "Would you like help?"

"I know how to do the assignment, it's just hard for some reason."

"I didn't say you didn't know how to do it. I'm just asking if you'd like help getting the focus to finish it." His persistence was admirable.

"Sure. What have I got to lose?" I shrugged, looking him in the eye. Scooting his chair over to me, Justin picked up my assignment to examine it.

"Mr. O'Reilly, may I ask what you think you are doing?" Mr. Fout's monotone voice floated over his crossword puzzle.

"I'm trying to help Robin with an English assignment. She's having difficulty getting started." Justin grinned at the drill instructor.

"Just keep it down." His attention quickly ran back to its puzzle, and that was the end of that conversation.

I was amazed at what had transpired. Did Justin really break one of the rules to detention? He wasn't being quiet, and he was interacting with another student. I couldn't believe that Mr. Fout had really let him get away with that! Maybe detention wasn't as bad as I had originally thought it was…

Looking back at the desk, I smirked at the paper. The ease of the assignment glowed with a renewed vibrancy. Quickly, the fervent velocity took over. Without thought or guidance from my newly acquired "instructor" my pen danced across the page, leaving its legacy for all to gaze and admire.

Upon completion, I read over what my pen had proclaimed. It was barely legible, but coherent. "Thank goodness," I thought to myself. "Rewriting it clearly shouldn't take that long."

Taking out another piece of paper, I copied the heading. No sooner had I started writing the structure for the outline than Justin's voice shot at my ears.

"You're doing another assignment?" He asked, tilting his head to the left.

"No." I said, shaking my head. "I'm writing this one over."

"Why?" His eyebrows scrunched together in a puzzled stupor.

"So it's legible." Unblinking, I gazed back at his confusion. My reasoning was obvious to me, and yet, was lost to him.

"Oooookay…" His reply came slowly.

Like a hummingbird darting from flower to flower, my eyes relayed the message Father Time proclaimed. It was 11:14am. 10 torturous minutes had tolerably drifted by. At that news, my stomach growled in anticipation of Mr. Fout taking our lunch orders. Innocently, I stared at him. My eyes opened widely, imitating a deer caught in a pair of headlights.

"Okay, everyone. Show of hands who would like a PBJ sandwich." Mr. Fout said, looking up from his crossword puzzle. Some kids raised their hands, and the prison guard took count.

"Now, who would like a bologna and cheese sandwich?" Mr. Fout counted the remaining hands.

My stomach sank as my nose wrinkled in disgust. Those were the lunch choices? Those were awful!

"You're not eating?" Justin pouted at me, saddened at the thought of me going hungry.

"I can't eat PBJ. I'm allergic to peanuts." My nose remained wrinkled.

"What about bologna and cheese?" Justin suggested.

"I'm lactose intolerant, and bologna is so greasy that it makes me sick to my stomach." The corners of my dimples sagged, revealing my broken heart at the loss of my beloved manna. "If there was something else to eat, believe me, I'd eat it. I'm starving."

"Mr. Fout? Is there anything else to eat for lunch?" Justin whipped around in his desk, taking the guard by surprise.

"No, there isn't Justin. What's the problem with the choices you have?" Mr. Fout's monotone wavered, and a slight hint of irritation could be heard.

"Nothing's wrong. Robin's allergic to peanut butter and cheese. She can't have either." Justin's chivalric actions made me blush.

"Then it looks like she doesn't get a lunch."

"Are you serious? You can't NOT feed us! Isn't there a law saying that the schools have to feed us?" Justin's response was delivered incredulously.

"Actually, the law says we're supposed to supply the students with meal options. If in the event that they're allergic, it is up to the parents to make special accommodations." Mr. Fout's attention returned to his crossword puzzle.

"Could you ask the cafeteria for just a jelly sandwich?" Justin asked, his tone returning to its natural soft gentle nature.

"No, Justin. The sandwiches come prepackaged."

"That's crap!" Justin fumed, allowing his distain to spew out his throat.

"If you don't like it, you don't have to stay Mr. O'Reilly. You don't have detention today. No one is forcing you to be here." Mr. Fout's arrogance floated over his puzzle.

"Don't worry," Justin whispered to me. "I'll bring you a lunch tomorrow. What do you like to eat?"

His generous offer caught me off-guard. What did I like to eat?

"I don't know. Let me think about it," I said, shrugging my shoulders and shaking my head. My stomach growled louder in protest.

"Sounds like you shouldn't have to think too hard," Justin grinned.

I just rolled my eyes, shaking my head some more. I guess he heard my stomach's vocal complaints.

"Well, I like mashed potatoes." I offered.

"Yeah? What else do you like?" Justin grinned.

"I like biscuits." I grinned back.

"Anything other than carbs?" He replied, laughing.

"Not really." I crinkled my nose in dislike. I wouldn't say that I didn't NOT like the other food groups, but I definitely favored carbs. Any pastas, breads, potatoes… anything like that, and I went absolutely gaga. I could eat 5lbs of mashed potatoes at Thanksgiving, take a nap, and wake up just to do it again. My family and my doctor didn't understand it. My doctor said it wasn't normal, but it wasn't unhealthy. He said it was just how my body worked. My metabolism processed carbs faster than it did any other food group. I always found that funny. I had heard that carbs were the longest molecules and took the longest to metabolize, and yet, my body could burn right through them.

"You don't want a cheeseburger?" Justin asked.

"Ew, no!" I replied, pulling the corners of my mouth down in a frowning pout.

Justin laughed. "I didn't think cheeseburgers were that bad!"

"They're not bad. I just don't like them. They're greasy."

"So you like carbs? You're not really picky on which kind of carbs. Just carbs in general right?"

"Yep." I nodded.

Our small talk was interrupted by a lunch lady walking into the room with a tray of food. There were several sandwiches and a piece of paper. Placing the tray on Mr. Fout's desk, she waited. Examining the paper, Mr. Fout gave her the appropriate money needed to pay for the sandwiches.

"Okay, come get your sandwiches. Form a single file line." Mr. Fout's monotone broke the silence. Everyone rushed up to his desk, everyone but us. The lunch lady left as silently as she had entered, not saying a word.

Heartbroken, I watched everyone receive their lunch. Everyone except me. Sighing, I looked at the clock. It was 11:28am. 12 minutes left. I sighed again and turned my back to reality, staring at my desk. I didn't want to be confronted with everyone else eating. Normally, I wouldn't have cared. But I was deprived my manna. Why should I watch them enjoy theirs?

"Robin?" Mr. Fout's monotone called to me.

"Yes?" I turned around to face him.

"I normally don't do this, but you may be excused early." Mr. Fout said.

"Ok, why?" I replied. Duh. I should've been grateful being allowed to leave 10 minutes early. Why did I ask why?

"See if you can go down to the cafeteria and find something to eat."

"Thank you." I replied, rushing out the door. I didn't want to continue that conversation, and I didn't want to stick around long enough for him to change his mind. With Justin at my heels, we rushed to the cafeteria.

Immediately, I recognized the lunch lady that had served the rest of my detention mates. I offered her a half hearted smile.

"What can I get you dear?" She asked.

"Could I have a couple slices of bread or a roll or something please?" I asked. I didn't want to be difficult, but I couldn't help it.

"How about a sandwich?" She asked with a smile.

"No thank you. I'm allergic to peanut butter." I wore my half smile for the time being.

"So how about just a jelly sandwich?" She raised her eyebrows, as if to suggest rebellion.

"You can do that?" My shocked reaction made her laugh.

"Of course I can. I don't see why not."

"Well, Justin asked Mr. Fout if you could do that for me, and he said no." I replied incredulously. I was furious at having been denied food and freedom, only to find out that I could've eaten at the same time the rest of the prisoners did!

"Mr. Fout is a jerk. He doesn't like to put any more effort in than he has to. Any time you need a special order, just let me know in advance. I wouldn't want any of my students to go hungry." She smiled, handing me a jelly sandwich. I tore into it with the voracity of a child at Christmas.

Closing my eyes, my tongue caressed the wave of deliciousness that flowed over and around it, into its crevices along every centimeter of my mouth. Ecstasy welled from my soul, engulfing me in a moment of pure heaven. Reality faded off into the background, becoming a not too distant memory.

"Thanks! I have detention tomorrow. Can I have a jelly sandwich?" I smiled at her with a mouthful of jelly.

"Sure dear. Do you want any milk or chips or anything with it?" She asked, taking out a pen and paper.

"Um… can I have orange juice?" I asked, swallowing my bite.

"You really should have milk in your diet." She stared at me with motherly disapproval.

"I would, but I'm lactose intolerant." I smirked sheepishly. I felt bad for superseding her authority, but at the same time, I knew she wasn't familiar with my allergies. To avoid an allergy attack, I had to supersede her.

"Ahhh. Then orange juice it is." Smiling, she handed me a pint size cardboard carton with orange juice.

"Thank you <u>so</u> much for the jelly sandwich and the orange juice." I grinned back at her.

"You're welcome dear. I'll see you tomorrow then." Smiling, she disappeared into the back room.

"Well that was nice of her," Justin said. His cheerful expression indicated that he had caught the smile that the lunch lady had infected me with just moments ago.

Without warning, the bell sounded. That meant we had four minutes to get to 6th period class, or else be tardy.

"Damn it!" I thought. "And I haven't even gotten a chance to touch my orange juice!"

"Hey, I got to get going to math. I'll catch you later." Justin waved, jogging down the hallway. Standing there, I realized that I didn't have my afternoon books and that I had to quickly finish my drink if I had hoped to make it to study hall.

Sighing, I knew that it was going to be a long rest of the day.

October 17, 2006   3:12pm

So detention sucked. Don't get me wrong, at least I got some of my homework done early. I still have more to do though. But I don't want to. NOT being able to eat sucked. And the detention teacher is an ass! His name is Mr. Fout, and he's such a jerk! He tried telling me that the cafeteria wouldn't make me just a jelly sandwich. Come to find out, yeah they would. In fact, they made me one when I asked for it! I told the lunch lady that I was allergic to peanuts, and she took the peanut butter off. Ooo, that was so hard. It's such an easy concept that even a monkey could understand it! Apparently, Mr. Fout isn't as smart as a monkey! Anyways, Justin was there with me today. It wasn't too bad. I wonder if he'll be there tomorrow. Who knows? As for right now, I'm hungry. So I'm going to go eat. I'll write more later.

Chapter 13

Scrounging around through the cabinets on my hands and knees produced fruitless results. What felt likes hours (but was probably closer to 15 minutes at the most), I looked, pulled cans and condiments aside, dug around, moving goods from the front to the back, the left to the right, and back again. Absolutely nothing jumped out at me, striking my fancy. A rumble could be felt throughout my torso, originating from my empty tummy.

Slowly, inch by inch, I had scoured every cabinet, every shelf. The only things I found half way interesting were a bag of tortilla chips and a can of condensed minestrone soup. Not a very healthy lunch or late lunch or snack or whatever category of meal it fell into, but it was better than nothing.

Stalking the stove, I impatiently waited for the soup to heat up. No matter how quickly I shoveled chips in my vortex of a mouth, they never reached my stomach. The grumbling continued, and my brain never informed the peons to deliver the message of "full".

The entire house was quiet, except for the "crunch, crunch, crunch" of the chips against my teeth. The stillness irritated me. Usually, it was a welcomed sign of peace. For some reason, it was not welcomed by me.

Looking inside the pot, I could see small bubbles starting to form. "Good," I thought. "Since it is starting to boil, it should be done soon." My stomach gurgled at the thought of eating soup.

Spinning around, I walked over to the cabinet that had the dishes in it. Grabbing the largest bowl we had, I went over to the drawer with the utensils. I pulled out the largest spoon available.

Pouring all of the soup into the bowl, I ate standing up next to the stove. With my left hand, I reached over to turn the stove off. With my right hand, I tried to shovel in the soup. When my left hand had returned to me upon completion of its task, I told it to fetch me some chips. My appendages were working double time to feed my dilapidated stomach.

I hadn't even noticed the contents of the bowl until I heard a familiarly disappointing sound, the sound of the spoon hitting an empty bowl. Saddened, I turned my attention to the bag of chips. That too, was almost empty.

"Crap. There's nothing to eat," I fumed to myself. I had no intention of ceasing my activities, but being unprepared made the continuation a bit of a challenge.

Imaginary bullets dropped me to the ground, to my hands and knees, as I quickly resumed my rummage through the cabinets. This time, I wasn't going to stop until I had found enough food to eat to satisfy my hunger for the rest of the night.

Amidst my quest for nourishment, I heard the door slam. While the sound had penetrated my auditory ossicle, my brain had failed to translate the message in time.

"Hey Good Looking. Whatcha got cookin'?" My mom's voice greeted me from several feet above. I recognized the words she said from a song she occasionally sang around the house. Some song from the 1940's.

"Hey mom." I replied from inside the cabinet.

"Whatcha doing'?"

"Looking for food." I said.

"Well, I can have dinner ready in half an hour. Why don't you wait until then?" Mom set her purse down on the table.

"What's for dinner?" I inquired, placing my upper torso into the majority of the kitchen. Looking up, I gazed at her expression. I knew what it said before she translated it for me.

"What would you like for dinner?" Tilting her head to the left, mom smirked at me.

"Mashed potatoes and chicken gravy!" I cried, a huge smile forming on my face.

"What vegetables would you like with it?" A belligerent mom expression joined her smirk. She may have found my deplorable eating habits to be cute, but the mother in her insisted on veggies.

"Aren't potatoes a vegetable?" I asked, trying to squeak by.

"GREEN vegetables! Try again." Sternly, she reiterated.

"Um...Hm... I don't know."

"How about brussels sprouts?" Mom grinned.

"No, mom. Every time you cook those things, the whole house smells for the rest of the night. It's awful." I crinkled my nose at the thought of that atrocious smell.

"Then you pick a veggie. If you don't, I will. And you know what I'll pick."

"Damn you! That's cheap. If I don't pick, then you're going to make the whole house stink!" I glared at her playfully.

"That's right." She glared back with a smirk.

"Fine." I sighed, giving up. "What about green beans?"

"Works for me." Mom bent over, picking up a can of canned green beans. Putting my soup pot in the sink, she began to open the can.

"How was school today honey?" Mom asked over the noise of the electric can opener.

"It sucked. How was work?" I asked.

"It sucked. Why did school suck?" Mom replied.

"Lunch detention sucked. My detention teacher sucked. Why did work suck?"

"My boss is an idiot. He sucks!" Mom shook her fist, making me laugh. Plus, our constant use of the word 'suck'.

Mom had an interesting way of getting her points across. Rather than lecture or nag or complain about the language we used (unless it was truly vulgar, then she would snip at me to stop), she would use it too. The more she didn't like the word, the more she would use it. The more we heard it, the more unintelligent the conversation sounded, until nothing important was being said. After a while, I would understand this and try a different way to communicate.

"Okay, babe. What did your boss do to upset you?" I smiled.

"Well I was on my way out the door to lunch and Richard yelled at me for not giving him the spreadsheets he wanted. But I did! I emailed the spreadsheets to him. When I told him that, he didn't apologize. He just said, 'oh'." Mom hissed.

"What a jerk. That wasn't very nice of him." I scowled.

"I know. What about detention upset you?" Mom asked tenderly,

"Well, for starters, they won't let you eat lunch until the very end of detention. So I was hungry right from the beginning! But they only serve pbj or bologna and cheese sandwiches! And when I asked the teacher if I could have only a jelly sandwich, he said no! So I didn't order lunch. So after detention, I went to the cafeteria, and this lady there said, 'yeah sure you can have just a jelly sandwich!'" I scowled again.

"Maybe he didn't know dear." Mom replied thoughtfully.

"No, mom. He didn't even call the cafeteria and ask them. He just said no." I grumbled. "His name is Mr. Fout, and he said it was the school's responsibility to give you a lunch, not to make sure you'd eat. So if you're allergic to peanut butter, you're S.O.L." SOL was an expression my dad used to say before he left. It meant Shit Outta Luck.

"Maybe you could bring a lunch tomorrow." Mom replied.

"I could. Let's see if there'll be any mashed potatoes leftover." I grinned.

"See? Problem solved." She smiled at me. How naïve of her.

"Yeah." I replied sarcastically.

"What else is wrong?" Mom asked, frowning at my lack of enthusiasm.

"It's detention. What would be right about it?" I asked, furrowing my eyebrows in confusion at her.

"Well, it's something you have to do honey. You may not enjoy it, but you won't enjoy everything you do in life."

"I know mom. It still sucks."

"Everything sucks!" Mom cried, throwing a fist in triumph over her head.

I couldn't help but laugh.

Sitting down to dinner was a wondrous distraction from the impending torture. I didn't want to think about having detention tomorrow. For now, I was focusing on the moment of dinner and enjoying it with my mother.

Placing a bite of mashed potatoes in my mouth, I closed my eyes and let my tongue experience the different tastes and textures of the carby goodness. Drifting away, I slowly moved the food around in my mouth without a care in the world......

October 17, 2006   8:14pm

So I didn't get any more of my homework done. Oh well. I don't really

care. I'll do it tomorrow. At least mom was more relaxed about me having

detention. God, she pissed me off yesterday! She had no idea why giving

me detention was bullshit. I don't know if she gets it yet, but at least she

understands that I'm not happy about it. Hopefully, it goes better

tomorrow. I have mashed potatoes for lunch. That's better than nothing

(which is what that stupid midget teacher would like to give me!).

Chapter 14

Standing in the halls, I looked around at my peers. With a slight sense

of avidity, I awaited my second day of lunch detention. Don't get me

wrong, I wasn't happy about doing it. Knowing that it wasn't as bad as I

had originally anticipated it to be made it a little easier. Plus, today I had a

lunch. Today, I had manna.

Taking my seat in my first period class, I ignored my surroundings.

Instead of paying attention to the other students trying to navigate around

each other in an awkward adolescent dance, I focused on making the most

out of study hall. Not that it mattered. Whatever I didn't finish now I could

finish in my second period study hall. Or lunch detention. My normally

reverent attitude towards the every day quotidian homework and excelling

in academics became placid. Nonetheless, I began where I had left off the

day before.

After completing my biology questions, I nonchalantly stared at my

assignment book. There wasn't much scribbled in it. Had I neglected to

write down my assignments? Or had my professors gone easy on this poor unfortunate soul? I had a nagging feeling I was forgetting something, but I couldn't place it.

"Oh well," I shrugged. "I'll remember it. I'm sure."

Drifting off into a day dream, I squandered the remainder of 1st period study hall and the entire 2nd period study hall. Only when my subconscious signaled that it was time to go to Mrs. Grant's class did I autonomically move. Like a well stringed marionette, I skittered from class to class. That is, until the end of biology had approached and my brain snapped on.

"It's time for lunch detention," a voice in my head told me.

"I know," I said.

"I'm just making sure you're aware." It replied casually.

Sighing, I grabbed my homemade lunch from my locker and sprinted towards detention.

Upon arrival, I saw his familiar face sitting at his usual throne.

"Good morning, Ms. Edwards." His dry monotone voice came from behind his daily puzzle. His pen moved across the attendance sheet.

"Good morning, Mr. Fout." I walked through the room, taking my seat in the corner. No matter what class I was in, I always sat in the corner. It was my way of hiding, of being out of the way. It was my protection measure. If I was far enough away from my peers, maybe they'd leave me alone. Wishful thinking.

Placing my lunch on the corner of my desk, a voice startled me.

"What is that?" Mr. Fout's voice contained a notable amount of irritation.

"It's just my lunch," I innocently replied. Like a scared rabbit, I curled up in my chair.

"From home?" He asked.

No, dumbass. I picked it up from a drug dealer before school. Hey man, it's just a little pot. My inner voice sneered at the stupidity of his question.

"Yeah." I spoke softly. As other students arrived, their eyes focused on the conflict between the child and the adult.

"Pass it up here." Extending his hand, Mr. Fout demanded my lunch. Handing it over, my heart thrashed against my ribcage before finding a spot to shatter inside my chest.

"In detention, students are only allowed to order lunch from the cafeteria." Mr. Fout spitted out more arbitrary rules.

"Why?" I asked. I wasn't trying to sound condescending. I was genuinely confused.

"Too many students were bringing in 'special brownies.' So now, the only option is to order lunch from the cafeteria." Mr. Fout explained.

"But it's not a brownie. It's mashed potatoes." I said innocently. I still failed to climb aboard his "logic train". From where I was standing, his train completely missed the station altogether!

"This isn't up for discussion, Ms. Edwards. In fact, you can go speak with Mr. Mitchell about it." Mr. Fout looked at me, unblinking. His small stature did nothing to diminish his intensity.

Sighing, I picked up my belongings and headed to the principal's office. I could hear Mr. Fout on the phone. Probably to his office to make them aware of my arrival, no doubt.

I trudged down the corridor, the (maybe) 50 feet to his main office. I hadn't gotten my entire frame in the room before I saw Mr. Mitchell.

"In my office," Mr. Mitchell said. I could tell his tone wasn't a happy one.

I couldn't understand what the problem was. Why was everyone making such a fuss about mashed potatoes?

"Mr. Fout tells me that you are being disruptive and breaking rules." Mr. Mitchell said. Staring at me, waiting for a response, I blinked.

"Is that true?" He continued.

"No, sir." I whispered. My heart was beating faster than I could breathe. My whole body stood as still as it could, hoping I could escape the whole ordeal with minimal damage.

"What is this matter of a lunch?" He asked, still sounding irritated. His hands clenched each other so fiercely that his knuckles turned white.

"I didn't eat lunch yesterday, so my mom made me a lunch for today." I said. I blinked again.

"Why didn't you eat yesterday?"

"Mr. Fout said that we could choose from pbj or bologna and cheese. I'm allergic to peanut butter and cheese. Mr. Fout said that the cafeteria wouldn't make a special order. He said the sandwiches come

prepackaged." I repeated Mr. Fout's horrendous starvation tactics.

"Well, as it is, students are not allowed to bring in lunches from home.

In the past, we've had too many students try to smuggle drugs into the

school." Mr. Mitchell lectured matter of factly.

"I didn't know that. I'm sorry," I softly spoke sadly.

"Well, now that you know, I assume you won't be bringing in any

more lunches to lunch detention." His tone eased up, as if the end of the

battle were drawing near.

Sure, and I won't eat. You people are assholes! Nice to know you care

so much about your students, you heartless bastard. My inner voice

hissed.

"Yes sir. Hopefully, I won't have any more detention!" I smirked,

trying to lighten the mood.

Laughing, Mr. Mitchell replied, "Yes, that would be nice. Alright, run

along to detention."

"Yes, Mr. Mitchell. Sorry to bother you!" I smiled, standing up.

Taking my leave, I slowly made my way back to lunch detention. I was in no hurry to see that tyrant who had stolen my manna, my heart, for two torturous days in a row. My soul and my eyes raced to the floor in a heartbreaking race, to which there were no winners.

Like a sweet serenade my devil whispered, *To hell with them. They can't treat you like this. It's inhumane. Don't go. Walk towards the door, and walk home. Just keep going.*

Sighing, my heart ached to follow the direction of my Id. But my superego screamed out the repercussions before I had a chance to entertain the notion. Taking my seat in detention, my stomach mimicked the sound of a low thunder roll off of the horizon.

I hope you're happy being hungry, Id grumbled. *They don't care if you eat. They don't care about you...*

That's not true, Superego interrupted. *They have rules to follow. That's all it is.*

Oh, bull. It wouldn't kill them to get you something to eat. But they're not going to do that. Why would they? Id snapped. *I'm hungry!*

You can eat when she gets home. You're going to have to wait. You have to finish your two days at detention. That's what we get for her walking home. Superego replied.

Would both of you shut up? Ego snapped. *Geez, it's like listening to two kids in the back seat! Just be quiet! Fighting isn't going to make this any better.*

Closing my eyes, I tried to tune everything out. Ignoring Mr. Fout's scratching pencil, I tried to remember a time when I was happy.

If you think about happy memories, it'll help pass the time and provide a good distraction. My ego tried to play mediator.

"I don't have any," I whispered.

Then think of happy possibilities, Ego whispered back.

Drifting away, I went home. Thinking about all the things I could do there, all of the food I could eat, all of the hours I could sleep away, made my heart heal. As a smile crossed my heart and my face, reality shattered my world of possibilities.

"Here are the lunch orders, Mr. Fout." The lunch lady said as she entered the room. Setting the tray on his desk, she reached for a particular sandwich.

Sauntering over to me, she smiled. "And here you go, dear. A plain jelly sandwich."

"Thank you," I smiled back, accepting her graciousness.

"Excuse me?" Mr. Fout's eyes raged with the angry fires of hell.

"She's allergic to peanut butter. You can't honestly expect her to eat a pbj, now can you?" The lunch lady calmly spoke to the dictator.

"It is not my problem what she's allergic to." Mr. Fout's face hardened. The only expression was the ire in his eyes.

"Well, I'm not going to let the little one starve," she called over her shoulder as she headed out the door.

"What the hell do you think you're pulling?" Mr. Fout jumped out of his desk, sending his chair crashing into the wall.

"Nothing," I whispered. Terror tied me to my chair, and his gaze might as well have been coming from Medusa.

"I have <u>had</u> it with you, Ms. Edwards! Leave! Go to Mr. Mitchell's office NOW!" he shrieked.

With tears in my eyes, I once again slinked out the door to the main office. Without a sound, I stiffly made my way back.

Not having reached my destination made no difference. Mr. Mitchell graciously ran towards me in the hall, eagerly awaiting my arrival.

"What is going on with you, Ms. Edwards?" He said, losing his composure. Throwing his hands over his head, the once professional overseer of the student body mimicked the movements of a monkey at a zoo.

"Nothing," I softly answered. A lone tear ran across the prairie, resting at the corner of my frown.

"This is unacceptable! You cannot do whatever you feel like! This is detention! This isn't tea time with the royal council! You were given options as to what you could eat! How dare you disrespect me and my staff!"

"I'm sorry," was all I could muster.

"Come with me. We're going to my office. I'm sure your mother will be thrilled to pick you up." Grabbing my book bag, he walked with me.

I sat in silence even after my mother had arrived. The two of them shared a private moment behind closed doors. When that was over, they bombarded me with questions. My only reply was to shrug and stare at the floor.

"What is going on?" Exasperation crashed against her voice. Standing next to Mr. Mitchell with her arms folded across her chest, she waited for an answer.

I shrugged.

"I didn't hear you," mom said.

"Nothing," I said.

"What happened with the lunch I gave you?" Mom snapped.

"Nothing," I echoed. By this point, I wasn't going to argue. Whatever it took to make the fighting stop was what I would do. Regardless if they didn't have the facts, I wasn't going to fight. What was the point?

"Talk to me," my mother urged. I didn't know what the facts would've gotten her, but I wasn't going to argue. If she wanted to know what happened, fine. But she couldn't hold me responsible if she didn't like what she heard.

"What?" The word shot off the end of my tongue.

"What is going on?" Mom asked.

"I don't know," I replied with a sigh.

"Well, tell me what happened."

"I went to detention and Mr. Fout freaked out about me bringing a lunch. Something about other students putting drugs in their lunches, so you're only allowed to order it from the cafeteria. Then the lunch lady brought me just a jelly sandwich, so he threw me out." The words tumbled over each other to get out of my mouth.

"Well, that didn't make any sense. Did you know not to bring a lunch?"

"If I knew, I would've mentioned it last night." I retorted.

"So why did he get upset about the jelly sandwich?" Mom asked. Her tone indicated that she was obtaining peace through knowledge.

"He thought I was getting special treatment. I wasn't. I didn't ask her to make me a special lunch. She offered to yesterday. And now Mr. Mitchell thinks I'm doing whatever I want…"

"That's not true." Mr. Mitchell interjected.

"Did you say that to her?" Mom asked incredulously.

"Yes, I did. I apologize. You can't pick and choose who you let follow the rules. All of the students must follow them." He recited an arbitrary rule.

"If I make her a lunch and she can't eat that, and she can't eat a lunch from the cafeteria, then what do you expect her to eat?" Mom snapped.

"Surely she can find something in the cafeteria to eat." Mr. Mitchell's composure had returned. Mostly.

"Like what? Because Mr. Fout threw her out for ordering a jelly sandwich. So I ask again. If she can't eat a homemade lunch, and she can't order something from the cafeteria, then what pray tell would you have her do?" Mom asked. Judging by the straightness of her mouth and the roundness of her pupils, she was about ready to snap.

"How about we call it a day and discuss this some other time? I know you are on your lunch break and I would hate for you to be late to work because of this 'meeting'." Mr. Mitchell's voice matched the monotone expressiveness of Mr. Fout's.

"What time would you like to meet tomorrow, then?" Mom asked, sighing. She was done with the battle, but she wasn't done with the war.

"How does 1pm sound?"

"Fine. We'll see you then. Come on, Robin. We're going home. Come on. Let's go," mom said. Without looking behind her, she stalked out the door. I quickened my stride to keep up.

"Well, we're going to have to straighten this out tomorrow." Mom said, navigating through the corridors towards the parking lot.

"Yeah, but I don't know how." I sighed again.

"If you didn't know the rules, then you weren't trying to break them." Mom offered encouraging words. That was just like her, to try to look for the best in every situation.

"I know. I mean, what do they want me to do? Not eat?" I grumbled.

"Oh, I'm sure they're not trying to starve you. They just have rules to follow. They're so used to kids breaking them for all the wrong reasons that when a student breaks them for the right reasons, they don't know how to handle it."

"I don't want to go back. I just want to go home," I said with a pout.

"Okay. Just don't forget. We have a meeting with Cindy tomorrow. We have to go over the details of the incident so she knows which charges to file. It's at 9am. Okay, pumpkin?" Mom smiled, tousling my hair.

"Okay, babe." I smiled back.

October 18, 2006 1:16pm

Why does every day have to be a battle? What is wrong with these people?

Every damn day I go to school, it's a problem, or an issue, or some other

bullshit. What the hell? I'm just trying to get through high school! I'm not

a bad ass trying to break the rules! Ooo, look at me! I know what'll piss

everyone off. I'll bring in a lunch so that I can eat! Yeah, that'll stick it to

them! I don't think so! I get to school at 7:30 in the morning. I get home at

3 in the afternoon. I just want something to eat at lunch! Hopefully, mom

can fix this. She has a meeting with the asshole principal tomorrow. Mom

and I have a meeting with Cindy tomorrow, too. She told me today that we

have to go over the details of what happened so Cindy can file the right

charges. Whatever. I just want this whole thing to be done and over with.

I can't believe I have 3 ½ more years of this shit… how am I going to

survive?

Chapter 15

"Come on, brat!" A voice chirped at me from the kitchen.

Rubbing my eyes, I looked at the clock. 8:12 am. Trying to find my way through the fog that had set in my brain, I remembered something about a meeting at 9 am.....

"Coming," I called back. I didn't want to hear more yelling. At least, not first thing in the morning. Throwing on a pair of pajamas, I flew down the stairs. Following the palatable and delectable aroma of brewing coffee Arabica led me to the secret location of my mother.

"We have to leave in 10 minutes. Make sure you're ready to go." Mom said from the paper.

"I'm ready now," I replied, slipping on my slippers.

My response prompted erupting laughter. "Are you really going like that?" Mom asked.

Looking down, I quickly examined my appearance. "Yeah, why not?" I asked.

"What happened to clothes?" Mom laughed some more.

"I'm wearing clothes." I scrunched my face in disapproval of her disapproval.

"No, you're not! You're wearing pajamas!" She corrected.

"Same thing." I said.

"Go upstairs and change into something nice. We're going to talk to a prosecutor, not going to a sleepover. Hurry up!" Mom called after me as I ran up the stairs. She had a point, but still. I felt most comfortable in my pajamas.

Bursting into my room, I ripped off my current wardrobe selection in favor of something more "mom-approved". This included a pair of jeans and a black tank top.

Rushing downstairs, mom nodded. That is, until she saw my feet. I hadn't even noticed I was still wearing my slippers.

"Oh, for heaven's sakes! Just put sandals or something on." Mom shook her head at me as she headed towards the car.

Stepping into my sandals I followed her movements, hoping it would lead me to the same end result as her. As we both climbed into our respective sides of the car and simultaneously shut our doors, the car

began to move with the ease of a figure skater.

To cope with the silence, I stared out the window. I watched the winds

and the trees dance a provocative dance with each other. It was

fascinating. First, the wind would dip and twist, pulling the leaves and

branches around and about. Then the trees would respond to the wind's

movements, completing the seductive Latin tango between them.

I was oblivious that we had arrived to our destination until I heard mom

slam her door.

"Are you coming?" She asked, gaining yardage on me. Quickly, I

scrambled out of my seatbelt to possess the ability to tailgate her.

Sprinting up the stairs of the courthouse building, I looked up at the

remainder of the architecture. Its archaic features were gray, with pithy

pillars that loomed over you. Commanding attention and respect, it eerily

stood there like a personal soldier to aid in the war on crime.

In silence, we waited for the elevator to take us to our destination.

Cindy's office was on the third floor. When the doors released us, we were

greeted by a receptionist.

"Good morning. May I help you two ladies?" She smiled at us.

"Hi, yes. We're here to see Cindy at 9am." Mom smiled back.

Looking at her appointment book, the receptionist narrowed down the appropriate time slot. "Ms. Edwards?"

"Yep, that's us."

"I'll let her know you're here." Picking up the phone, I can only assume the person that she was speaking to was Cindy, she announced our arrival.

"She'll be right out." Just like that, we had completed our interaction with the seemingly friendly receptionist. Her smile had disappeared as her attention wandered back to her computer.

"Good morning, girls." Cindy's face lit up like a college student's at spring break when she saw us.

"Good morning," we chorused back.

"Shall we retreat to my office?" Cindy chirped. Heading back the way she came, we followed suit.

Her office was lavish, right down to the cherry wood table with the plush office chairs. There was an oriental style rug underneath it. There were a couple people already seated. I recognized Sgt. Saroka. I didn't

recognize the man in the dark suit.

"Have a seat, ladies." Cindy took her own seat.

"This is the assistant district attorney, Mr. Clements. Mr. Clements, this

is Annette Edwards. Her daughter, Robin, is the girl I told you about. I'm

sure you two remember Sergeant Saroka." She passed around

introductions, and small talk was immediately exchanged.

"Let's cut to the chase." Cindy interrupted, taking out a notepad and a

pen. "We were discussing the charges and the evidence. So far, we have

pictures, doctor's reports, and two complaining witnesses. We also have

an admission from the perpetrator."

"Yeah, but because she's under 18, she needed her guardians present.

We had to throw it out." Mr. Clements grumbled.

"True, but we're doing pretty good without it. I'm confident we can

win this case." Cindy smiled. We smiled back. "What we're going to need

from you today is to go over your story again. We have to make sure the

defense attorney doesn't have any way to mess this up."

"Okay," I replied, swallowing.

"Okay, let's go over what happened from the beginning." Cindy was

poised and ready to pounce on her notepad.

"Well, after 4th period, I went to my locker. I have lunch 5th period. I

always switch my morning books for my afternoon books, and then go to

the cafeteria to eat lunch. This way, I'm never late for 6th period." I began.

I could see Cindy writing furiously, and Mr. Clements was hot on her

writing trail.

"I had just put all of my morning books in my locker, when I felt

someone push me from behind...."

"How do you know it was someone pushing you? Maybe someone

accidentally bumped into you?" Mr. Clements scrutinized me.

"I felt a hand on my back, just between my shoulder blades." I reached

around, pointing to the spot.

"Continue, dear." Cindy cooed.

"Well, when I was pushed, I ended up falling into my locker, hitting

the corner against my eye." I folded my hands perpendicularly, indicating

the position of the locker, and where I had made contact.

"When I looked up, I saw a group of cheerleaders walking past me, laughing." I finished.

"How did you know which cheerleader it was?" Mr. Clements asked.

"I don't, for sure. I think it was the one with the curly hair, the one whose locker was right next to mine. She was always kicking my books down the hallway and being really nasty." I nodded, insisting on my point.

"Has she ever been physical with you before?" Sgt. Saroka piped up.

"No. I mean, she's kicked my stuff around and slammed my locker shut, but this is the first time she's ever done anything to me." I shook my head, shrugging my shoulders.

"Have you ever been physical with her before?" Mr. Clements asked.

My eyes popped out of my head at that question. "No!"

"Never? Not once? Not even on accident?" He pressed.

"Never! I've never hit anyone, never, not once, not for any reason." I shook my head, my eyes still opened incredulously.

"Just asking. If there has been a history of violence between you two, this may not be anything different. But if this is the first incident of violence, and she's the one that perpetuated it, then the jury will think you're more innocent." Sgt. Saroka explained. Gently, he put his hand on my arm.

"But I am innocent!" I said, shooting straight up in my chair. My spine had been jerked by the invisible hand of righteousness.

I must've said something comedic, because all of the adults started to laugh under their breath.

What did I say that was so funny? I asked myself. I didn't find the truth to be humorous. It was what it was.

"Has anyone seen her kick your books or slam your locker shut?" Mr. Clements asked dryly.

"I'm sure someone has," I replied.

"Anyone in particular?" He pressed.

"The other cheerleaders. They've been around her when she's done that."

"Anyone else?"

"I don't know." Annoyance resonated in my voice. I hated being asked the same thing over and over again. Asking the same thing ten times wasn't going to change my answer.

"We just want our own witnesses. The defense is going to use the other cheerleaders to back up the one being charged," Cindy soothingly said. Poor thing, trying to mediate between a frightened adolescent and a grouchy old codger.

"Do I need a lawyer?" The question darted out of my mouth before I was even aware it had formed in my mind.

"No, dear. I am your lawyer," Cindy smiled at me, affectionately reaching for my hand. "I may be a district attorney, but I am your attorney. I represent your best interests."

Blushing slightly, I felt a little foolish. Smiling back, I nodded in understanding.

"Does anyone have any more questions?" Cindy asked, looking around. Nobody spoke, at least not at an audible level.

"Okay, then we're adjourned." Pushing up from the table, Cindy gathered her things. The sound of wood scraping wood became apparent as everyone followed her lead.

I walked with mom back to the car in silence. Glancing at the clock on the wall, it said 11:35am. We had time to kill before the meeting with Mr. Mitchell.

The sun felt warm as it attempted to penetrate my sweater. My skin wanted to reach up and return its warm greetings, but the looming sense of nippiness in the air stopped the friendly union in its tracks. Anyone could feel the yearning the two had for each other, like long lost high school sweethearts at their 50th reunion. Sighing, I longed for the "good old days" of summer.

"So what's the game plan?" I asked mom.

"Well, I have that meeting with Mr. Mitchell at one. Do you want to come?" Mom returned my question with my question.

"Not really." I crinkled my nose.

"Okay, so then how about we talk about what resolution you would like to this lunch fiasco, and I'll take you home." Mom smiled at me.

"What about school?" I perked up at the prospect of missing school.

"You're sick. Poor thing." She grinned at me.

I grinned back, my heart soaring. I was just told that I can miss school, and that mom will back me up on it! Nobody could give me detention for this absence!

"Eh, he. Eh, he." I faked coughed, trying to conceal my smile. It worked until we made eye contact. That's when we both started laughing.

"Oh, you're so funny!" Mom playfully smacked my leg.

"So what is Cindy going to do now?" I asked. It had slipped my mind to ask what the next step was at the meeting.

"Well, my guess would be that she's going to file the charges and we're going to receive notice to appear in court. The cheerleader will receive the same papers, except she's going to be the one facing the charges." Mom informed me thoughtfully. I wasn't sure if she knew for certain, but she sounded confident.

"Okay."

"So, let's talk about lunch." Mom eased her foot on the brakes, slowing the car down to match the red light.

"What about lunch?" I asked, puzzled.

"Well, Mr. Mitchell is upset about you in lunch detention."

"I know."

"Do you know why?" Mom asked.

"Kind of." I replied.

"Well, tell me what you know." Mom said, switching pedals.

"Mr. Mitchell and Mr. Fout said that students aren't allowed to bring in homemade lunches because kids in the past would put drugs in their lunches. I told them I didn't do that, but they didn't care. Then they said I could get either a pbj or a bologna and cheese sandwich. So I said I'm allergic to peanut butter and I'm lactose intolerant. They said it wasn't their job to accommodate to my allergies. They only had to supply me with a lunch." I recited Mr. Mitchell's and Mr. Fout's blasphemy.

"Well, from the options they're giving you, it's either starve or get sick." Mom grumbled. She didn't like the scenario any more than I did.

"What can we do?" I slightly shrugged. I wanted to do something, but adults didn't seem to take in the advice or words of an adolescent.

"Can you live with just a jelly sandwich?" Mom asked.

"Yeah," I replied half-heartedly. It wasn't as good as mashed potatoes, but it was better than nothing.

"Good. Because they're going to let you bring in a lunch from home or a jelly sandwich. Those are the options, and they have to live with it just like we have to live with it." Mom jabbed her head down, trying to emphasize her "I have spoken" mind frame.

I could see its beauty from 50 feet away. There it was, my home, our home, elegantly poised for entry. There was something magical about its presence, as if it commanded everything around it to cease function. Its owners were home, and for a moment, it appeared that the Venetian blinds wiggled in excitement from inside the house.

"There you go kiddo. I'll give you a call as soon as the meeting's over." Mom reached over and kissed my head.

"Okay, love you!" I hugged her back, and ran towards my warm and loving domicile.

"Love you too!" She called out. I could hear the revving of the engine as mom sped away. I didn't care. I was home!

October 19, 2006   12:07pm

Well, the meeting with the district attorney is over. I guess everyone

wanted to go over what happened again so they can get the paperwork

right, or whatever. Cindy was there. She's pretty cool. Sgt. Saroka was

there. He was a lot quieter today. There was some other guy. He was an

ass! He attacked me like I did something to deserve this or I somehow

made it happen. He can kiss my ass! Anyways, mom is on her way to go

talk to Mr. Mitchell. I hope he stops being so stupid. Seriously, I'm going

to put drugs in my lunch? I don't think so! I'm hungry. That's why I eat. I

don't eat to get high. Duh. Drugs are gross. People who smoke pot are so

stupid. They laugh at everything, even when it's not funny. There's this

kid that has the same lunch period I do. I swear, he's always stoned. He's

always laughing the most retarded laugh at the stupidest things. Anyways,

I'm going to go watch TV until Mom calls me and let's me know what

happens.

Chapter 16

The inside was eerily quiet as I navigated around the kitchen. I was
hungry and on "the hunt." My eyes narrowed as tunnel vision took over,
leaving my olfaction in charge.

After what seemed like hours (but was probably closer to 15 minutes), I
gave up hunting. It was proving to be fruitless, so I yielded to the desire to
mindless entertainment. To the idiot box I went!

Flopping down on the couch, I turned on the television. I
absentmindedly flipped through the channels, staring at the generic images
bombarding me until I heard the door.

Like a dog, I immediately perked up. Not having watched the clock, I
was unaware of the serious lapse in time.

"Marco!" I called out anxiously. I was hungry, and I knew mom could
fix it.

"Polo." A weary voice replied.

"How'd it go?" I asked, arising from the couch.

"Well, you get jelly sandwiches if you ever have detention again. And you have one more day of detention." Mom flopped down next to me.

"Why?" I whined. Her words slapped me across the face.

"Because the second day of detention you had, I ended up taking you home. So you still have to do the second day." Sighing, she slipped out of her shoes.

"Okay…" I understood, however thrilled I wasn't. "So, what's the plan?"

"You tell me."

"I'm hungry."

"So go to the kitchen and get something to eat." Mom said.

"There's nothing to eat." I frowned.

"Oh, of course there is. You're not looking hard enough. Stop being picky and only looking for carbs. There's plenty of stuff to eat." Picking herself up, she sauntered over to the kitchen with me at her heels.

Beginning her own search, mom was having as much luck as I had.

"Get in the car." Mom stood up from the cabinets on the floor.

"Where are we going?" I asked, feeling dumb the second the question left my mouth.

"Grocery shopping. Where else do you buy food?" Mom smiled at me, tousling my hair with her hand.

"Rock on!" I grinned, racing to the car.

I loved grocery shopping. Looking at all of the food, all of the endless possible recipes, made my heart and my stomach mimic the circular movements of an acrobat.

I heard the click of the seatbelt as I fit the safety key in its lock. I looked up just in time to see mom by the driver's side door.

"Come on!" I grinned, urging her to make haste.

"Shad dap!" Mom threw nonsensical words in my direction. I laughed. Nice to see she was lightening up.

After a few moments of movement, I turned on the radio. Mom always had her car tuned to a "light" radio station, and some romantic 80's ballad I vaguely remembered hearing years before started to play.

"Do you have a list?" I asked.

"Do you have a list?" mom echoed.

"No." I replied. "No, wait! Yes I do!"

"Do NOT even tell me the entire store!" Mom raised her voice in a humorous, cautionary tone. I cracked up laughing.

"You are incorrigible!" Mom laughed with me.

"It was worth a shot." I shrugged, still grinning.

"Seriously. What are we buying? Because I do not want to buy the whole store." Mom's voice was a little stern.

"Um... we need milk, and eggs, and egg noodles..." I began.

"Do you want any soup or anything?" She asked.

"I don't know. You're the boss." I shrugged again.

"Okay. Mush." Mom made a whipping motion with her hand, and I laughed. She was such a riot!

When we got to the grocery store, the parking lot was about half full. *Thank goodness,* I thought to myself. *At least it's not too busy. I don't want to deal with a lot of people.*

My gait had a slight saunter as we perambulated through the store. Very few things could comfort me the way sleep did. Food was one of them.

Walking side by side with mom through the aisles, I took in the visual stimuli. Even though I wasn't eating, seeing all the food transported me to another world. I was so far away, that I was completely unaware of what was about to happen…

As we walked through the soup aisle, hands suddenly grabbed my sides from out of nowhere. Terror gripped me as I felt fingers lock into my ribcage. My heart skipped a beat as the "fight or flight syndrome" kicked on in my head. I could see mom to my left, so I knew it was a foreign entity. But who?

As I turned towards the approximate location of the stranger, I could hear laughter. Confronting the person who had terrorized my safety bubble brought an unexpected surprise.

"Fancy seeing you here," Justin grinned, his hands returning to his own side.

"Hey!" I gushed, throwing my arms around him in relief. Knowing the threat was a false alarm brought my vitals slowly back to normal. "What are you doing here?"

"It's senior skip day. A bunch of us are getting snack food to watch movies all day. What are you doing here?" Justin replied with the same impish grin he always wore.

"Just grocery shopping." I replied, mimicking his grin. "Mom, this is Justin. He's in my gym class. Justin, this is my mom." I stepped aside, waving my hand in conjunction with the introductions.

"Nice to meet you," mom said, extending her hand. Something was wrong. I could see it on her face, but I couldn't figure it out...

"Nice to meet you too." Justin shook mom's hand. "Well, I'd better get the popcorn. I got peeps waiting. Catch you later!" Justin waved as he jogged off.

"You know him from school?" Mom said, raising an eyebrow.

"Yeah. He's in my gym class." I replied, my voice light hearted.

"Just be careful." Her words were cryptic. Their true meaning eluded me.

"Why?" I asked.

"He should be in school." She picked up a couple cans of soup off of the shelf and dropped them in the cart.

"It's senior skip day, mom." I replied, rolling my eyes.

"So I heard."

"What's wrong mom?" I asked. Her demeanor nagged at my heart.

"I'm just saying, be careful. I have a bad feeling about him." Pushing

her cart ahead, I knew she didn't have too much to say on the subject.

"I will, mom." I said, letting it go. I followed her around the rest of the

store in silence, only making small talk as far as inquiries about groceries

were concerned.

When we had arrived back home, I piled my arms with as many

grocery bags as I could carry inside. It was our "thing". I brought them

inside, and mom put them away. When the last bag had found its way to

the kitchen, I retreated to my thoughts.

October 19, 2006   3:47 pm

Mom and I went grocery shopping. We ran into Justin. He scared the crap

out of me! I didn't even know he was there! He said it was senior skip

day, and that's why he wasn't at school. It's kind of weird, because I

thought he said he was a junior. Whatever. Mom met him. She didn't seem

too thrilled. I don't know why. Every time I ask her, she just says, "be

careful." Be careful of what? He's not that bitchy cheerleader! He didn't

hurt me! She did! Anyways, mom talked to Mr. Mitchell. I guess they're

going to make me jelly sandwiches whenever I have detention, which is

only one more time. I guess because mom took me home yesterday, they

want me to make up that day of detention. After that, no more! I'm going

to make sure I don't get any more detention! That sucks! That's a bunch of

bull crap! It shouldn't be a battle to eat lunch! Jackasses! Oh well.

Anyways, I'm going go find something to eat. I'm starving!

Chapter 17

Despite being at school the next day, I was in a surprisingly good
mood. Having an unexpected day of respite from this mandated prison was
always an occasion worth being happy about. I had spent the previous day
with my mom, laughing and eating. There was no reason to be upset or
stressed out. I had no experience with my horrid peers and their evil ways.
I had had a good day, and had left my worries at school.

I was eager to see Justin in gym class. Our surprise run-in the day
before while grocery shopping had temporarily lifted my spirits. I had kind
of hoped that seeing him in gym class today could produce the same
results.

Scanning the room, his auburn curls stood out from the crowd. As a
grin swept across my face, my feet danced their way over to him.

"Hey!" I called out to Justin, smiling.

"Hey you! Long time no see!" He grinned back, helping me close the
distance between us. This time, it was he who threw his arms around me

for a hug. In an autonomic response, my arms wrapped themselves around his broad muscular torso.

"Yeah, I know!" I replied, still smiling. "So how was the movie fest yesterday?"

"Great! We watched a bunch of thrasher movies. It was great! There was blood and guts all day long!" He grinned.

"Awesome! My favorite kind of movie!" I laughed.

"So did you really skip school yesterday just to go shopping?" Justin asked, raising an eyebrow skeptically.

"Nahh," I shook my head. "Mom and I had a meeting with the DA yesterday."

"How'd that go?" He asked, slightly surprised.

"Fine. They went over what happened, so they could file the right charges or whatever. I guess she confessed, but because she wasn't 18, they had to throw it out. They said if she doesn't take a plea, then we're going to trial." I shrugged.

"So I heard." He nodded. I wasn't sure if he nodded in agreement with what I had said, or if what I had said confirmed what he'd already knew.

"So you've heard? Wow, word travels fast. Especially because you're the first person I've told." I grinned.

"A lot of the other kids are talking about it. I know Stacey's very upset about the whole thing." Justin said.

"Who's Stacey?" I asked, crinkling my eyebrows in confusion.

"The cheerleader?" Justin asked, almost rhetorically. He acted as if I should've known that.

"That's her name?" I asked.

"Yeah, why? What did you think it was?" He laughed at me.

"I didn't know, honestly." I shrugged. "Why? What is she saying about it?" Curious minds wanted to know.

"Well, I guess she doesn't want to go to trial, but she doesn't want to plead guilty. She says she didn't mean to hurt you."

"Then why did she push me?" Anger spat my words out, as his words slapped me in the face. Did he really know that heathen? Was he fraternizing with the enemy?

"Oh, knowing her, she was probably just goofing around." He shrugged.

"Funny." I said through clenched teeth.

"Hey, now. Don't let her get to you," He said, rubbing my shoulder. Glancing at his hand on my arm made my anger ebb away.

"Come on, O'Reilly! Move it, or I'll mark you absent!" His gym teacher snapped from across the room.

"Got to go." Vanishing like the Cheshire cat, leaving his smile to dissipate last, he trotted over to his side of the gym.

Wandering over to my own herd, I could see that my gym teacher was planning on dividing the class into two teams. I wondered what physical activity we would be commencing in.

"Okay. Today, we're going to be playing baseball. There will be two captains, and your captains will take turns choosing members of their teams. Do we have any volunteers?" The teacher announced.

I groaned inwardly. I hated baseball. While I loved watching sports, I hated any sport that had anything to do with physical contact. For example, it was terrifying to me trying to have the bat make contact with the ball. It was even scarier when it did. Unfortunately, I couldn't obtain credit just sitting on the sidelines. Man, that would've been nice!

As I looked around the room trying to determine which corner I could

slink away to, female chatter whizzed past my ear.

"I hope we don't have HER on our team. She'll probably go whine to

the other team about what we're doing. That's what rats do." Her venom

spat. Turning around, I looked at the source of the voices. The expressions

on their faces showed no remorse. Instead, justified anger and hatred

perched itself on their shoulders. Their words punched me in the stomach.

How could they be so cruel?

Looking at the teacher, I could see she was still taking attendance. Had

she heard what these vultures had said? No, apparently not. She didn't

bother looking up from her clipboard.

I just sighed. If I told the teacher, then it would prove those two harpies

right. I'd only be a rat. If I didn't say anything, then anyone could say any

hurtful thing whenever they wanted without fear of repercussions. What

was a girl to do?

Distancing myself from reality, I numbly walked to the outfield. If the

teacher didn't care enough to do something about it, then I wasn't going to bother. Besides, "ratting" them out would only cause retaliation, and I was anticipating enough retaliation from the trial.

For forty minutes, my class went about their business around me. Even if the ball went into 'my' area, I knew I could count on some boy to come running in after the ball. They were passionate about sports, and their passion pushed them to win the game.

By the end of class, I was thoroughly depressed. My good mood had been slain by the harpies' cruel words, and I knew the worst had yet to come. I had lunch detention today. There was no way out of it.

In a zombie like state, I managed to survive 3rd and 4th period. When the bell to 5th period rang, my stomach seized. All of the bells and alarms went off in my head, signaling danger. It was time to face detention. I hadn't seen Mr. Fout since he flipped out on me and sent me to Mr. Mitchell's office.

Between the potentate's words and the impending doom, depression and fear gripped me.

It would've been different if I had a friend to talk to, but I didn't. I had me, myself and I. If I had a friend to talk to, we could've discussed it and forgotten it. Instead, their vicious words replayed over and over in my mind. In the end, all I had were their vicious words and my mind to talk to.

I hate this place, my Id whined. *I just want to go home.*

Just go and get this over with, Superego snapped back. Groaning, I trudged my feet to detention.

Walking in the door, I could see Mr. Fout with his usual crossword puzzle. Looking up at me, he didn't seem too pleased.

"Welcome back. Did you straighten everything out with Mr. Mitchell?" Cockiness rang his vocal bells. I could only assume that he secretly wished for me to get more detention. Not because he wanted to see me, mind you, but because he thought I should suffer.

"Yes," I replied, taking my seat. Turning my back towards him, I stared at the desk. There was no food, no manna, sitting before me. Just an empty desk covered in scribbles that had been so generously left by previous persons.

I tuned out Mr. Fout's voice as he recited the rules for any possible newcomers. Wanting nothing more than to escape, I rummaged through my book bag for any possible distraction. Coming up empty handed, I

took out a piece of paper.

Looking at the clock, it read 11:03 am. "38 minutes left," I thought to

myself. Writing out the numbers between 1 and 38, I decided to cross off

the numbers as the minutes went by. It wasn't the most exciting thing to

do, but it was something. I couldn't convince my soul to become

passionate about homework, and I couldn't feed my body. The only thing

left was my mind.

At the usual time, the lunch lady arrived with her tray of pseudo-

manna. She placed a sandwich in front of me.

"Here you go, kiddo." With a smile, she left.

Upon examination, I could see it was a plain jelly sandwich. Nothing

special, but it was better than nothing. Shrugging, I undid the shrink wrap.

"What do you have there?" Mr. Fout's acrimonious question distracted

me from the shrink wrap.

"Just a jelly sandwich," I shrugged off its importance.

"Well, isn't that special?" Mr. Fout seemed annoyed at the "special"

treatment" I had received.

My heart sank a little further in my chest as I slouched in my seat. What was his problem? Why was he upset about me getting a sandwich?

I decided to draw out the eating process as long as I could by taking slow deliberate nibbles. I was going to attempt the largest distraction I had ever ventured to take. It took my whole being not to inhale this simplistic nourishment, but I managed to savor ever bland speck of its existence.

"You may go." Mr. Fout's voice interrupted the last two bites. The other students quickly ran out of the room. Shoving the remainder of my sandwich in my mouth, I snatched up my book bag.

"Ms. Edwards?" Mr. Fout said, looking at me.

With bulging cheeks, I blinked my eyes. It would've been rude to verbally respond with my mouth full. Plus, I didn't want to risk losing any food to the floor.

"How did the meeting with Mr. Mitchell go?" His haughty tone angered me as I swallowed the contents of my mouth.

"Fine, I guess. He said that when I have detention, I get jelly sandwiches. I just can't bring in a lunch from home." I shrugged. Having not been at the "meeting", I could only speculate as to what my mother and Mr. Mitchell said. While mom had reported the end results to me, I

still didn't know what happened from beginning to end.

Disappointment spread across his face. He seemed mad that an

adolescent had managed to circumvent the rules. Nodding, he seemed to

accept the end results.

Hey, asswipe. I don't want just a fucking jelly sandwich for lunch. I

want a real lunch! I don't get what I want, you don't get what you want!

We're both miserable with the decision, so quit your bitching! Id screamed

at him. Thank goodness I was the only one to hear such harsh words.

"Get going to your next class," Mr. Fout said. His voice matched his

facial expression, and I was grateful at the reprieve. Scooting at the door, I

didn't even bother with polite pleasantries. I was on the warpath, running

in any direction that would take me away from that monster!

October 20, 2006   2:48 pm

Holy shit! Thank god today is over! School was horrible! First, some bitch

in gym class said I was a rat because of what that cheerleader did. I knew

that the other students would be upset, but they have no right to say

anything about it! I hate that! I hate it when other people say things about

what's going on. If they're not going to help make the situation better,

then shut the hell up! All they're doing is making it worse! And Mr. Fout

is such a jerk! He seemed pissed off that I got a jelly sandwich for lunch

detention! I shouldn't have even had detention! I showed up Tuesday for

the second day! He's the one who threw me out and sent me to Mr.

Mitchell's office! It's not my fault I wasn't in detention the whole time!

Oh well. I'm done with detention! I'm never going back there again!

Besides, I'm home now. I get to actually eat something, <u>anything</u> besides a

jelly sandwich!!

Chapter 18

Wandering around the prison yard like a convict, I made my way around to the side door that I exited in the afternoon. I had never attempted entry from an exit before, but there was a first time for everything.

Standing outside the door, I tilted my head back at the structure. Looking at the 3 story brick building, I sighed. It may have looked like a school, but it felt like a prison.

Pulling on the handle bar that went across the length of the door produced no effects. *Crap,* I thought. *It must be one of those doors that you have to push open from the inside.*

Sighing again, I walked around to the front door. Aside from the main entrance, there were two side entrances. Having no luck with one of the side entrances would lead me to believe that I wouldn't have luck with the other side entrance.

Can't we just go home? Id whined, its childlike pleas stabbing my heart like a dagger.

We could, and get in unnecessary trouble. Superego bantered back.

What if she threw up? Then we could go home. Id offered.

She's not sick. And she can't throw up on command. Superego gritted

its teeth.

There has to be something! Id continued whining.

Yeah, there is. Shut up and deal with it! We're already at school. Might

as well get it over with! With that, superego had won the daily argument.

Sighing, I arrived at the threshold of hell. Every part of my being

wanted me to run, run as far and as fast as my tiny body would carry me

off into the distance. Hanging my head down in defeat, I walked inside the

flames.

After so many years of "school", it was getting to be a bit much. It

wasn't the mandated boring classes, although they didn't help. It was the

continual crap from my peers. Sure, the days of rest were nice. But they

were so few and far between that it didn't justify returning. At least, not

anymore.

A little less than four years. Then I can go to any college I want, and I

won't ever see these jackals again. I cooed to myself, petting my breaking heart. Wandering around the halls, I made my way to my locker. The cattle herds went about their business around me, as if I didn't exist.

I suppose I don't exist to them, I shrugged to myself. *Oh well. If they would just leave me alone all together...*

Lowering myself to my knees, I leaned in my locker. Mindlessly, I began to switch my afternoon books for my morning books. That's when I heard the giggling. Unlike normal giggling, this giggling didn't stop.

After a few seconds, I paused my morning rituals to survey my surroundings.

"Hey, rat girl." It was the same girl from gym class.

I just stared at her.

"Did you just call her 'rat girl' because she's ugly?" Her friend was on the verge of cracking up.

"No, because she's a snitch. But now that you mention it, she IS ugly." The first girl laughed hysterically, causing her friend to lose composure.

Rolling my eyes, I turned back into my locker. I could hear them laughing as they walked away. Holding my breath, I tried to prevent the tears from escaping. I didn't want to advertise that my heart was breaking.

These vultures didn't need any invitation to hurt me further, and any sign

of weakness would've been perceived as one. As fast as I could, I pushed

the pain down to the bottom of my soul. Maybe a little too fast, because it

left a vacuum that rage eagerly filled.

Standing, I gritted my teeth and slammed my locker shut. *Looks like*

it's going to be another one of those days, Superego sympathized.

Clenching my jaw, I marched along to the tempo of the rage that built

inside of me. The beating drums grew louder and louder with each passing

step.

They wouldn't find it so funny if it was happening to them, Superego

grumbled.

Maybe we should show them how it can hurt. Id's wicked grin was

enticing, and I perked my ears up to hear Id out.

That wouldn't be very nice. Superego scolded.

And what they're doing is? Id snapped back.

I'm just saying, if we can get through the rest of high school, then we

don't have to deal with this ever again. Superego sighed.

And I'm just saying, hurt those bastards. Let's see how they like it.
Maybe shoot the school up like they did in Colorado. Id grinned wickedly.

Absolutely not! Now shut the hell up! Superego screamed in
discomfort. While I understood both sides of the argument, I decided to try
and survive the remaining 4 years without committing any egregious acts.
Regardless of how they hurt me, I didn't want to hurt them. I didn't want
to be like them. Even though the idea <u>was</u> tempting…

Taking my seat in homeroom, my vision blurred. I was angry, and it
was all I could focus on. "Hey, rat girl." Her words sloshed around in my
mind, dousing gasoline on a smoldering decade of pain.

In an unconditioned reflex of my neck, I tried to shake the negative
feelings away. It wasn't even 8am, and if I didn't abandon the events, it
had the ability to ruin my whole day.

Closing my eyes, I breathed deeply. For five minutes, I concentrated on
my breathing. *Breathe in, breathe out.* I told myself. I continued my
pseudo meditation trick until my umbrage subsided.

Hearing the seats shift, I opened my eyes. The other students were heading off to their respective classes. Wiggling free of the desk, I followed the pathway to my first class.

Study hall. While it wasn't important, I was glad to have it first thing in the morning. I was still tired, and if I had no work to do, I could put my head down on my hands and sleep. I could trust the bell to wake me up and instruct me to head to my next class, so it didn't matter if I was asleep or awake.

Settling into the chair, I looped my arms around my bag. Fluffing the bottom left corner, I curled my hands around the end and nestled my cheek against the makeshift pillow.

As I drifted off into happiness, a familiar voice disturbed me.

"Hey, it's rat girl." She whispered.

"Fuck off, bitch." I mumbled into my neck.

"What?" She asked incredulously.

I wasn't sure if she heard what I said or was just shocked that I said something. Either way, it didn't matter to me. Jerking my head up, I looked at her with complete ire. "I said, 'fuck off, bitch.'" I stared at her, unblinking. My heart pounded as our gazes locked. I wanted nothing more than to jump across this table and claw her eyes out. We were both the predator this time, standing in total statue form, neither side moving, waiting for the other side to attack first.

Her eyes opened wide. For a second, she was taken aback by my sudden spunk. "Oh really?" Glancing at her friend, they exchanged non verbal communication. Then she looked back at me. "You want to go?"

"Bring it." I replied, arching my back. My vision began to blur as ire took over once again.

"I'll show you who's a bitch." She pushed her chair back, causing the attendant to look up.

"Chelsea! Why are you out of your chair?" The attendant snapped. For study hall, we didn't have teachers. We had adults who monitored us, like attendants.

"She started it," Chelsea pointed her finger at me. My breath caught in my throat. Is she really trying to blame this on me?

"Both of you, up here now." Her voice grouched across the room. Pushing back my chair, I picked up my small frame and trudged to the front. I could feel my cheeks burning as everyone's eyes magnetically gravitated towards me.

"What is going on?" the attendant asked.

"She said, 'fuck off, bitch.'" Chelsea whined.

I gritted my teeth. *Cute how you FORGET to mention what you said, bitch.* I thought.

"Is that true?" She looked at me.

"She said, 'Hey, rat girl.' Again." I retorted.

"Okay, both of you to Mr. Mitchell's office. NOW." She pointed towards the door.

Sighing, I took my leave.

Get her! NOW! Nobody's around! Id screamed, jumping up and down like a crazed sports fan.

Oh yeah, that's a good idea. If it's only the two of you, and she gets her ass beat, then I wonder who did it. Superego yet again tried to wrangle control of id.

"Bitch." Chelsea swore at me.

"Yeah. **I'm** the bitch." I facetiously agreed.

Walking into the main office, I could see Mr. Mitchell's unsmiling face.

"Hello again, Ms. Edwards." He didn't look too happy to see me. I pulled the corners of my mouth upwards in a fake smile. "Have a seat. I'll talk to this young lady, first." He motioned Chelsea into his office. I nodded.

Sighing, I tried to think of the false spin Chelsea would put on it. I knew I was going to get in trouble. Every time I had been to Mr. Mitchell's office, I had received detention.

Now you're screwed. Id said. *You should've jumped her in the hallway.*

She started it. You can explain what happened to Mr. Mitchell. I'm sure he'll understand that you REacted, and that it was her who acted first. Superego was always the logical one. I just rolled my eyes.

After 10 minutes, Chelsea walked out. Her demeanor was nonchalant, and I received no clues as to the outcome of their meeting.

"Shall we?" Mr. Mitchell asked.

Standing up, I skulked once more into his office.

"Would you like to tell me what happened?" He asked, closing the door.

I shrugged. "She called me rat girl. Before homeroom, she said, 'Hey rat girl.' Then in study hall, she said it again."

"And what did you say?" Mr. Mitchell asked.

"Nothing." I said, only referring to this morning.

"She says you called her a bitch." Mr. Mitchell stared at me intently, trying to "spook" a confession out of me.

"My head was on my bag. I usually sleep in first period if I don't have any homework to do. Ask the attendant." I shrugged again.

That's right. Keep your mouth shut. It's her word against yours. If you don't tattle on yourself, then he can't prove you said anything. Id whispered into my ear.

"Were you going to fight her?" Mr. Mitchell inquired.

"No!" I replied, mortified. A felt a twinge in my heart as the lie left my lips. I knew that the anger would've controlled me, making me fight. But I had never gotten in a fight on my own accord.

Nodding, Mr. Mitchell seemed convinced. "Just stay away from her

from now on. I've told her to stay away from you. Understood?" I nodded,

grateful at not having received detention.

"Good. Now go back to study hall." With that, I had successfully

eluded detention. Walking down the halls with a smile on my face, I had

almost forgotten the morning in its entirety.

Taking my seat, I nestled my head back into my hands.

"Bitch," Chelsea cursed under her breath at me.

"Fuck off," I cursed back.

"You better watch your back." She vowed.

"Bring it."

The bell rang, reprieving me from her company. Wishing I had my

computer with me, I used an ersatz sheet of paper instead.

October 21, 2006 8:45am

That damn bitch from gym class! She called me rat girl this morning in the

hallway, and then in first period. I swear to god, can't these assholes leave

me alone? I haven't done anything to them! I just want to be left alone!

And the attendant actually thought it was my fault! Stupid bitch! They're

all stupid bitches! I had nothing to do with this! Although I did say, fuck

off bitch. It was kind of funny. "Chelsea" actually thought I was going to

fight her! I've never gotten in a fight in my life! Why would I start now? If

she's looking for a fight, she isn't going to find one here. What kind of a

name is Chelsea, anyways? I hope the rest of the day goes better. It's too

early for this shit....

Chapter 19

For the next forty minutes, I enjoyed the silence that accompanied 2nd period study hall. Nobody talked to me. Nobody bothered me. I was invisible and insignificant. I was in heaven. By 3rd period, I had a slight smile on my face. The tumultuous events that had transpired first thing were beginning to fade into the background of my mind, like a nightmare wearing off.

I managed to survive through the rest of my classes with a smile. When 5th period came, my soul nearly jumped out of my throat.

Lunch! Id squealed in delight.

Walk in a calm fashion to your locker, and get your afternoon books first. Superego mothered. Shaking my head, I smirked at their recent quarrel.

Pulling up on the lever to my locker, I swung open the door. Before I even had a chance to bend over, I noticed a black bottle on the top shelf.

That's strange. I never use that shelf. What the hell is that? I thought to myself. Reaching for the bottle, I could hear "shhh's" behind me. Ignoring it, I pulled it closer to my eyes.

On the label was a skull and crossbones. Above it read, "Rat Poison." Gritting my teeth, I put it back on the shelf. I turned around and saw Chelsea leaning up against a locker.

"Hey, rat girl." She said. Her face was motionless. Only her eyes revealed her anger.

Rolling my eyes, I walked past her. *Fuck this,* I thought. I threw my book bag in my locker and slammed the door shut.

What about lunch? Id asked innocently.

Shhh. Superego silenced Id, sensing the inappropriate timing of its question.

I continued walking down the hall. I had become completely unaware of my surroundings. The only thing I was concerned with was the side door. I wasn't about to stay and put up with this shit. If I left everyone alone, I was harassed. If I fought back, I was harassed. If I went to the adults, I was harassed. I couldn't win!

I kept walking. I walked all the way home, focusing everything on my destination. My mind, my vision, everything. I was angry, and scared, and everything in between.

October 21, 2006 11:17am

I can't believe it! That bitch Chelsea put a bottle of rat poison in my locker! I know it was her because she was standing there! She's been calling me rat girl all morning! She's pissed because I'm not going to take her shit anymore! I'm not going to take anyone's shit! I've had it! For 10 years, they've given me crap! I haven't done anything to anyone! When is it going to stop?! Is she really going to poison me? I'm going to have to find a way to protect myself, at the very least. But I swear, if this shit doesn't stop, I'm going to snap on everyone in that fucking school.....

Chapter 20

Taking a deep breath, the realization of trouble slowly crept up on me. I had skipped my afternoon classes, yet again. And yet again, I knew I would receive detention. For some reason, adults didn't care if the reason why you did something validated your actions. There was no justification. The world of right and wrong was as black and white as an old rerun on TV.

Sighing, I decided to beat the school to the punch and give my mother a call. I wasn't sure if they'd call her, but I'd be damned if anyone ratted me out before I did.

After two rings, I heard her perky voice on the other end. It warmed my heart and made me smile.

"Hello?" She asked.

"Hey mom." I replied. Sensing a confrontational moment, my nerves began to seethe with anticipation.

"Hey kiddo. Where are you?" She asked. There was a twinge of concern in her voice.

"I'm at home." I said, cringing.

"Why aren't you at school?" Now she was annoyed.

"Some girl started calling me rat girl. Then she put a bottle of rat poison in my locker." I said, wondering how much more I would have to say. Would she be on my side? Would she be upset somebody threatened her "baby"? Or would be just be mad that I had walked home?

"Did you see Mr. Mitchell?" She asked.

"Yes, but he thought I started it."

"Did you?"

"No!" I was flabbergasted that she would ask me such nonsense.

"Okay, start from the beginning." Mom said, trying to maintain composure.

"Okay, well I went to my locker this morning and some girl in my gym class started calling me rat girl. I didn't say anything. Now mind you, this is the same girl that said yesterday that she didn't want me on her team in gym because she thought I was a snitch and I would go to the other team. Well, she's in my first period study hall, and she started calling me rat girl again! I told her to leave me alone, but she stood up like she was going to fight me. That's when the teacher sent us to Mr. Mitchell's office. Neither

one of us got in trouble because it was 'she said, she said." So at lunch,

she was standing up against the lockers behind me laughing at me because

she put a bottle of rat poison in my locker!" I finished, taking in a huge

breath.

"And you didn't tell Mr. Mitchell what she had done?" Mom asked.

"No. I figured if she's serious about hurting me, then I'm out of there."

I smiled half heartedly.

"You need to tell Mr. Mitchell what happened." She lectured. "He

can't do anything about it if he doesn't know about it."

"What is he going to do? Give her detention?" Annoyance resonated in

my voice.

"I'm sure he'll do something. Why don't you go back to school and

talk to him?"

"Whatever." I said, rolling my eyes.

"I'll talk to you later. I love you." Mom said.

"Bye." And with that, I hung up. I wasn't going to talk to someone who

wouldn't listen to me.

Sighing, I ran my fingers through my hair. I knew in my heart that talking to Mr. Mitchell wasn't going to stop the other kids from starting trouble with me. In fact, the more I complained, the more trouble would come.

I have to find a way to protect myself. I thought. *Nobody is taking this seriously, and I'm not about to get hurt because they're too stupid to do anything about it.*

Moving the mouse, I double clicked the internet icon. I didn't have enough time to learn martial arts, and I needed a weapon. Being 14 might have stopped me from going into stores and looking, but no one could tell my age over the internet.

Typing in "protection" in the search engine brought an array of web sites. Too vast, in fact. *Maybe I should try a different search,* I pondered. This time, I tried "guns". The search was a lot more specific, but all of the sites required proof that I was 21 and older.

Sighing, I started surfing through the websites. I had no intention of going back to school to talk to the principal, and I had nothing but time to kill. Besides, if I couldn't protect myself with a gun, I had to find some way to protect myself, right?

I hadn't even noticed I clicked on a WWII informational website until I saw the photos. Even though they were black and white, you could see the horror and despair on the people's faces through the barbed wire fences, their frail and delicate frames pushing the remnants of their tattered souls. Beneath it was a caption:

"Chlorine gas was not a new weapon. However, never before had it been used in concentration camps. Very rarely were there survivors. People exposed to Cl2 experienced a variety of symptoms, including chest pain, vomiting, coughing, difficulty breathing, or excess fluid in their lungs, eventually leading to death."

Tilting my head to the right, a vindictive smile crept over my lips. *I may not be able to get my hands on a gun, but I'm sure I can get my hands on the stuff to make chlorine gas. That'll teach those assholes not to mess with me. That'll show everyone who's boss. Besides, I don't have to make the dosage lethal to do damage. I could release enough gas to make them sick. That'll teach them.* Id grinned.

You can't do that! Superego was mortified at the thought.

Yeah, because being nice and not fighting back is making them stop. Your way isn't doing shit. Id snapped.

But you can't hurt them like that! Superego quipped.

Want to bet? Like I said, I don't have to use enough chlorine gas to kill them. I could just use enough to hurt them. Id's malicious tone was rather enticing to me as I carefully absorbed every word. Listening to superego had gotten me nowhere. Now, I was starting to listen to Id.

October 21, 2006 12: 43pm

So I talked to mom. She wants me to go back to school and talk to Mr. Mitchell about what Chelsea did. Oh yeah, that'll fix it. Wait a minute. That bitch put a bottle of rat poison in my locker because the cheerleader that pushed me into my locker got in trouble. So if Chelsea got in trouble, who would threaten me to get revenge for Chelsea? Oh, you bitches didn't think about that, did you? Of course not. Why would you? You morons think there's only one way of doing it, and everybody follows the rules. You bitches don't know shit. Don't worry. I found a way that'll take care of everything. I'll show these mother fuckers who they're messing with. They'll leave me alone, trust me.

Chapter 21

The rest of the afternoon was spent day dreaming about ways to make

chlorine gas and get it into the school. What was it going to be like when

those noxious vapors caressed the interior of the demons possessing that

building?

I had lost all track of time until I heard the door. Glancing at the clock

told me it was time for mom to be home.

Quickly, I destroyed all evidence of mischievous activities and headed

downstairs. I hoped to persuade mom to see my side of the argument.

Hopefully.

Not that I was completely innocent in this situation. I wasn't saying that. I

was saying that I was the lesser of two evils, and I was tired of being

treated like I had equal culpability.

Slowly, I walked around the corner. Spying her I said, "Hey babe."

Turning around, she spied me. "Hey yourself. Did you go talk to Mr.

Mitchell?"

I shook my head.

"Why not?" Instantly, she was annoyed. This must've been a sensitive topic for her. I didn't know why though.

"Because." I replied, thinking it was obvious.

"Because why?" My obvious thinking didn't transcend to anyone else.

"What good will it do?" I was beginning to get annoyed myself.

"What did I tell you? Mr. Mitchell can't find the solution if he isn't aware there's a problem." She sounded irritated.

"Mr. Mitchell isn't going to 'fix' anything." I returned her irritation with my own.

"Why isn't he going to fix it?"

"Guaranteed someone is going to give me crap. First, it was the cheerleader. Then, when someone complained, she stopped. But Chelsea started giving me crap. If I complain about Chelsea, someone's going to get mad that Chelsea got in trouble, so they're going to take it out on me." I resisted the urge to roll my eyes at the obviousness at the situation. Why was I the only person to understand the hierarchy of high school?

"Well, skipping school isn't the answer." Mom said.

"I know."

"Then we need to come up with a better solution."

"I know."

"Well?"

"I don't know!"

"How about I set up a meeting with Mr. Mitchell for tomorrow, and the three of us can sit down and talk about it?" She suggested.

"Okay." I shrugged. I hadn't been able to come up with any solutions. At least, none that I was willing to share. "So what's for dinner?" I grinned.

"I just got home, and you're already bugging me!" She threw a pack of gum at me from her purse. I laughed.

"Seriously, what's for dinner?" Putting on my most serious face, I stared at her.

"Whatever you're making." She grinned at me.

"Macaroni and cheese it is!" I laughed.

Shaking her head, mom walked away. Rummaging around in the cabinets, I found a box of macaroni and cheese. Placing a pot of water on the stove to boil, a hand clasped its dainty fingers around the pseudo

gourmet dish.

"No way. If we're eating macaroni and cheese, I'm going to show you

how to make it from scratch. None of this boxed garbage." Mom shook

her head at me in disapproval.

Staring at her with mock disbelief, I said, "Well, then don't ask me to

make dinner! Why ask me to make something and then tell me no?!"

Rolling her eyes, mom shook her head again. "It's not that I'm telling

you no, it's that I would like to see you develop better eating habits. You

cannot go through life eating junk food. It's not healthy. Here. Grate this."

She handed me a cheese grater and a block of cheese.

"I like junk food, mom." I replied with a puppy face.

"I know, baby. I just want the best for you." She petted my hair.

"How do you know what's best for me?" I asked, not trying to sound

pretentious.

"I don't know for sure. I go with my gut." Mom smiled at me. "Am I

doing a bad job?"

"No, mom. I'm just saying. What if I think something is good for me, and you think it's bad?"

"That's a good point. But remember, I have 20 some years on you. I've been around the learning block, dear." She continued petting me as I kept grating.

"Is that why you keep telling me to talk to Mr. Mitchell?" I didn't mean to divert the conversation that way. My mouth spilled out the words before my brain could filter the words.

"Yes, partly. I think that since he is head of the school, he has the power to intervene. But if you don't tell him there's a problem, how is he supposed to fix it?" Mom pulled her left cheek upwards, giving me a lop-sided "I'm the mom, I know more than you" grin.

"True. If he doesn't know about it, he can't do anything about it. I'm just saying that even if he stops one student from giving me crap, someone else will…" I began.

"Language." Mom lectured with a glare.

"Sorry. I just meant the other kids won't leave me alone. I don't know why they can't all just leave me alone. They just won't. I've been in school for 10 years now and they keep harassing me. If someone gets in trouble, one of their friends will hurt me for their friend getting in trouble. It's not fair, but what can you do about it?" The realization of never being able to escape their hell marred my soul yet again. My exterior revealed flawless features, but my interior mirrored that of a war hero who made contact with a shrapnel bomb.

"Well, that's why we're going to talk to Mr. Mitchell tomorrow." Mom gave me an encouraging smile. I gave her a fake smile back, and returned my attention to dinner.

October 21, 2006   7:19pm

So mom's a little mad that I didn't go talk to Mr. Mitchell. She's going to

bring me to school tomorrow, and the three of us are going to sit down and

try to solve this. At least mom didn't argue with me when I said that if I

ratted on Chelsea that someone would take her place. For the time being, I

don't know what to do to solve it. Mom doesn't have a clue, either. I have

one idea though. Hehehehe…..

Chapter 22

As mom and I waited in Mr. Mitchell's office at 8 in the morning, a sense of fear came over me. My inner voice told me that the adults' methods of handling these "problems" were ineffective, and that anything they did now would yield fruitless results. I didn't know if they were clueless as to what was really going on, or didn't care. I just knew that what they had done in the past didn't help, and I had serious doubts about anything they would do in the future.

"Good morning, ladies." Mr. Mitchell's voice wafted over to us from his office door. Mom stood, and I followed. "Shall we begin?" As mom and I walked into his office, my head screamed at me, *Run!*

Taking my seat, I looked at the floor. I didn't think that the adults were going to talk to me, just around me. It was as if I didn't exist. What was the point of trying? Besides, their methods didn't work. I had found a method of my own that I was willing to try.

"So what seems to be the problem?" Mr. Mitchell asked.

"Well, Robin left school again at lunch. I guess she's being bullied by someone else." Mom said.

"Who's bullying her?" Mr. Mitchell acted concerned. My stomach somersaulted in my torso's pit. Who was he fooling? When that bitch gave me crap yesterday, he had no problem thinking I had something to do with it! Now that mom was here, he wanted to act like he cared? Give me a break!

"I don't know. Why don't you tell Mr. Mitchell what's going on." Mom nudged me.

"Some Chelsea girl. I don't know her last name." I mumbled, still staring at the floor.

"Is this regarding what happened yesterday?" Mr. Mitchell asked.

"Kind of." I replied.

"Did something else happen?" The same faux concern he chose to wrap his words in was starting to aggravate me.

"Yeah. She put rat poison in my locker."

"What?" I didn't answer his shocked question. I didn't think I was being funny, or that what I had said needed repeating.

"How do you know it was her?"

"Well, I went to my locker at lunch time to get my afternoon books, like I always do. When I opened it, there was a bottle of rat poison on the top shelf. I turned around, and she was standing behind me laughing at me."

"What did you do with the rat poison?" Mr. Mitchell inquired.

"I put it back in my locker, and left."

"So it should still be there?"

"Should be." I nodded in agreement.

"Well then, let's go have a look." Standing up, Mr. Mitchell led the march towards my locker. When he arrived, he waited for me to open the door and reveal its contents. Pulling open the door, everyone's eyes scanned the top shelf. There for everyone to admire its glory was the bottle.

Reaching up, Mr. Mitchell grabbed the bottle and brought it into ocular focus. I watched his facial expressions, trying to judge his reactions. Mom was trying to sneak a peek at the bottle for herself. Very subtly, Mr. Mitchell's face showed composure, then confusion, then indignation.

"This is unacceptable!" Mr. Mitchell spoke. Tried as he might, he couldn't keep his feelings under complete control.

"May I see it?" Mom asked, reaching for the bottle. Mr. Mitchell handed it off to her. Spinning it around, she examined the label. "This is some heavy duty rat poison!"

"Are you sure it was Chelsea who put it in your locker?" Mr. Mitchell asked, still very upset by the ordeal. I wondered what it was that particularly upset him. Was it the fact that one of his students was threatened, or that he was not able to maintain as strong of control as he had thought?

"Not 100%, no. But like I said, she was standing right there laughing at me when I saw the bottle at lunch." I pointed to the exact locker that she was cozying up to not 24 hours prior.

"Well, let's find out where she is right now and ask her." Mr. Mitchell started walking in the direction of his office.

"I know where she is," I offered. I kept my face placid while Id screamed with delight at the prospect of watching Chelsea writhe under pressure.

"Where?" Mr. Mitchell turned around, returning to the group of hens.

"In the cafeteria in study hall. We have study hall first period in there every day." I pointed in the direction of the cafeteria. It was getting harder and harder not to show my delighted anticipation. Somehow, I kept cool.

Mr. Mitchell walked down the hallway, his stride increasing. He wasn't in a hurry, no. He was on a mission! He was desperately trying to regain control of this rowdy herd of delinquents. *Good luck,* I thought dryly.

Bursting into the cafeteria, Mr. Mitchell said, "I need to speak with you outside in the hallway. Now!"

Chelsea's face went pale as her body slowly complied with his demand. Like a scolded puppy with her tail between her legs, she followed Mr. Mitchell to the hallway.

"Did you put this in Robin's locker?" Mr. Mitchell squeaked. His anger was getting the better of him.

"No." Chelsea replied, looking up from the floor.

"Then who did?"

"I don't know."

"Robin says you were standing at her locker when she opened it and that you were laughing at her. Is that true?" Mr. Mitchell was fuming. Without some kind of admission of guilt, he couldn't truly punish her. He wasn't interested in punishing her. He wanted order back in his domain. At what cost though?

"No." That was the only word in Chelsea's vocabulary.

"Liar!" I interjected. "You were standing behind me with the same girl you sit next to in study hall!"

"Should we bring her out and ask her?" Mr. Mitchell asked. A vindictive smile crossed his face as he felt order being restored to him.

Chelsea remained silent.

"Ms. Edwards, can you point out her friend please?" Mr. Mitchell requested. Walking over to the window of the cafeteria door, I pointed to a brunette who was focused on the door. Mr. Mitchell walked back into the cafeteria and returned with the brunette. Would her loyalty remain with Chelsea, or would the mousy brunette sell her friend out to save the remaining shreds of her own soul?

"Ms. Edwards says that you and Chelsea were involved in an incident at lunch yesterday concerning this bottle. Is that true?" Mr. Mitchell inquired.

"Yes." The brunette was intimidated.

"Did you put this in her locker?" he asked.

"No."

"Did Chelsea?"

"Yes."

"Did you see Chelsea put this in her locker?"

"Yes."

"When was that?"

"After second period." She responded. Chelsea gave her a quick look that said, "How could you?"

Looks like it's everyone for themselves, I thought with a grin.

"Tell me everything that happened." Mr. Mitchell said. His voice had begun to regain composure.

"Well yesterday during first period, Chelsea was calling her rat girl. And she said something in her book bag, but I didn't hear what she said.

So then Chelsea got all mad like she wanted to fight, and the attendant sent them both to your office. When Chelsea got back, she asked me to go to the store down the street with her during second period. That's when we picked up that bottle and put it in her locker." The brunette pouted slightly, her eyes protruding in sadness.

"You're saying you witnessed Chelsea put this bottle of rat poison in Ms. Edwards' locker?" Mr. Mitchell stated.

The brunette nodded.

"Okay, thank you. Please see me during lunch so we can discuss detention for skipping second period and for leaving campus. You may return to class now." Mr. Mitchell dismissed her, and the brunette scampered back into the safety of the cafeteria.

"Would you like to change your story, Chelsea?" Mr. Mitchell's smug grin was almost too much to bear.

"She cursed at me! She's the one that tried to start a fight!" Chelsea whined.

"I beg your pardon! My daughter doesn't fight!" Mom scolded, folding her hands across her chest. With mom's words, Chelsea looked as if she'd been slapped back in line.

"Chelsea, please gather your things from class and come with me to my office." With her head down, she walked back into the cafeteria.

That's right, BITCH. Do the walk of shame, Id cackled.

Shame on you. She's very scared right now! Superego scolded.

She should be. Dumb BITCH. Id grinned.

"I am truly sorry for all this, Ms. Edwards." Mr. Mitchell said to my mom.

"There has to be something we can do to keep my daughter safe." Mom said.

"Any time there's a problem, all she has to do it come tell me and I'll handle it." Mr. Mitchell smiled.

"My daughter doesn't think that'll work," Mom paraphrased my words.

"Oh? And why is that?" Mr. Mitchell asked me.

"Because Chelsea started harassing me when the cheerleader got in trouble. If Chelsea gets in trouble, someone will give me crap because she got in trouble. It's not going to stop." I replied sadly.

"Well, something has to be done. I will not tolerate this behavior in my school." Mr. Mitchell said. The door pushed open, and Chelsea reappeared. Her face was still pale, and her eyes were full of tears.

Poor child. Superego pouted. *She doesn't need to go through this kind of pain.*

Yeah, poor baby. Id hissed. *Why don't I bash 'poor baby' 's head against a locker. Then, you can give the bitch all the sympathy you'd like!*

You're evil! Superego spat.

Hey, whatever helps you sleep at night. Id shrugged.

Looking up at mom, I waited for her authority to tell me what we were doing next. Mr. Mitchell was busy walking with Chelsea, and Chelsea was living every second in agony until her parents were done reaming her a new one for her behavior.

"Shall we, babe?" I smiled.

"Shall we what? I'm going to work." Mom smiled back.

"Okay…" My smiled faded.

"Have fun in school, honey." Mom started to walk off.

"Why?" I whined in protest.

"Why what?"

"Am I staying here?"

"Yes, of course."

"Why?" I whined some more.

"The problem is solved. There's no reason for you to miss class. So get to class. Go on. Have a nice day dear." Mom smiled.

Not saying a word, I sadly watched her leave. I knew there was no point in arguing with her. She still didn't see things from my perspective, and my intuition said she wasn't going to anytime soon.

Returning to the scene of the crime, I bent over and scooped my bag up. Luckily, it still contained my morning books. Sulking back to my first period study hall, I kept my eyes on the floor. With each passing step, my heart broke a little more.

There is no way I can escape this hell, is there? I thought to myself.

Maybe not, but there is a way to make their lives the same hell as yours. Id grinned wickedly.

Would you stop?! No chlorine gas! Superego squealed.

And why not? Id challenged.

I don't see the other kids using chlorine gas to hurt her. Superego retorted.

Maybe it would be better if they did. Their words are their weapons, and words don't leave any visible marks. I commented.

Don't think like that. Just 3 and a half more years of this, and then you are free. You can go and do whatever you like. Superego could feel the battle being lost. That didn't stop her from trying.

Meanwhile, back in the REAL world, this shit has been going on for 10 years. Isn't that long enough? Id sneered. *10 years is more than long enough. I say we give them a taste of their own toxic medicine!*

Enough, you two. You're giving me a headache. Trying to push their recent conflict from the forefront of my mind, I pushed open the door to study hall. With everyone's eyes on me, I quietly took my seat.

"Ms. Edwards, do you have a hall pass?" The attendant barked.

"No, sorry." I called back.

"Go to the main office and get one." She commanded.

Sighing, I stood up and headed for the door yet again. The bell screamed overhead, signaling the end of 1st period. *Too late. It doesn't matter now,* I thought. *I'd better go get one and humor the witch.*

Trudging against the herd, I slowly made my way back to the main office. Upon entry, the secretary smiled at my return.

"Did you forget something?" She asked.

"My study hall teacher wants a hall pass." I grumbled.

"Of course." Scribbling on an orange piece of paper, she began filling out the necessary information. Turning my head to the left, I looked at Mr. Mitchell's office. I couldn't help but wonder what Chelsea was going through. Not that I cared or felt sorry for her. I just wanted to see what was happening.

"Here you go."

Extending my hand, I accepted the pass with a false smile. "Thanks." Turning around, I bumped into Sgt. Saroka.

That's right, bitch! You're lucky the cops are here to protect you! Otherwise, I'd shove that bottle of rat poison down YOUR throat! Id hissed.

"Hey. Long time, no see." I smiled up at him.

"How's it going, kiddo?" He smiled back.

"You know. Same shit, different day." I shrugged.

"Yeah, I hear you." He nodded slightly.

"You'd better go, dear. You don't want to be late for your next class." The secretary gently interjected.

Waving goodbye, I meandered down the hall back towards the cafeteria. That's when I heard the bell scream again.

Damn it! I thought. *Fuck! Now I'm going to be late for second period study hall. Just watch. This bitch will write me up for that. If she does, I swear, I'll bitch slap the stupid out of her...*

Gritting my teeth, I walked back into the cafeteria. Dropping the pass on her desk, I quickly turned my back towards the attendant.

"You're late." She snipped.

"Sorry. I had to get a hall pass for first period," I snipped back. Taking my seat, I looked up to meet her gaze. Surprise graced her face at my retort.

What the fuck you looking at, you ugly bitch? Id snapped.

Shush now! You don't always have to be so confrontational! Superego scolded.

Then tell that ugly wench to point her ugly mug in another direction! Id snapped again.

Sudden crackling brought everyone's attention upwards as the loudspeaker sprung to life.

"I apologize for the interruption. Instead of attending your normally scheduled third period class, we will be holding an assembly in the gymnasium. Once again, I apologize for the interruption." Mr. Mitchell's dry monotone voice flatly stated.

I wonder if this has anything to do with Sgt. Saroka. I pondered to myself. Not that I cared about particulars. It was just odd to have an impromptu assembly in the middle of the morning.

Patiently, the entire cattle herd waited for the bell to ring. Everyone wondered what the assembly would be about. Was it important? What was going on? Slowly the minutes ticked by, bringing us closer to our answers.

Within one minute of the bell ringing, I began putting my book bag back together. Creating a domino effect, the other cattle followed suit. Seconds before the bell rang, some of the cattle dared to get up from their seats.

Shrugging to myself, I thought, *When in Rome...* I stood up just as the bell signaled our attendance in the gym was mandatory.

Entry to the gym was slow as the entire student body tried to file in one at a time. Once the students had entered, there were clusters of peers waiting for their fellow kind to find them. Ignoring them, I chose to keep walking to the corner of the bleachers. Down in front and against the wall is where I always sat. This way, I was out of my peers' way. However, I was also in a direct line of vision for any adult that was policing the floors.

"Everyone find a seat." Mr. Mitchell commanded. Hearing his voice startled me, as his gentle tone had been replaced by an irate one.

Geez, something's got his hackles in a knot. I thought. Watching the students clear, I was able to see Sgt. Saroka standing at the podium with Mr. Mitchell. Chelsea was up there, and two adults (I assumed her parents) were with her. Whoever the guy was, he looked pissed!

"Everyone, settle down. I have an important topic to discuss." Mr. Mitchell said. Within seconds, the decibel level had reduced drastically, leaving only the hum of the generator to be heard.

"Thank you." Mr. Mitchell began. "I know everyone is wondering why I called an emergency meeting. In the past, we've only had assemblies if everyone was informed with at least a week's notice.

"However, there was an incident yesterday during lunch. That is why I have called this assembly.

"Yesterday, Chelsea Bingham decided to put rat poison in another students' locker. I do not know what provoked her to pull such a heinous stunt, but let me assure you. I will not tolerate this kind of behavior in my school!

"Hazing may not be illegal in this state, but let me warn anyone thinking of doing anything that can be construed as hazing. There are other laws to which Sgt. Saroka would be more than willing to charge you with.

"Sgt. Saroka, what could you charge Ms. Bingham with?" Mr. Mitchell smirked at him. Stepping aside, Sgt. Saroka and Mr. Mitchell traded places at the podium.

"Well, just for simply putting a bottle of rat poison in another student's locker, you could be charged with aggravated harassment. Aggravated harassment is an A misdemeanor punishable by up to one year of jail and a $1500 fine." Sgt Saroka informed us. Chelsea's face went pale as the prospect of jail time escaped the Sergeant's mouth.

"Thank you," Mr. Mitchell scooted towards the podium again to continue with his rant.

"If I need to ask Sgt. Saroka to monitor the halls and all student activity during school hours, then I will do so. I personally think you are becoming adults, and I would like to treat you as such. However, I will not have anarchy and chaos in my school! The choice is yours." Mr. Mitchell huffed.

Looking around, I could see much of the other students looking around in inquiry.

"So while I would like to treat you all like adults, I will ask the High Grove Police Department to monitor the halls for the next couple of weeks. Any suspicious behavior will be reported to me. The suspect in question will then be turned over to the proper authorities. Instead of detention, the suspect will be taken to the police station and dealt with accordingly." With Mr. Mitchell's conclusion lingering in the air, nobody moved. Nobody was sure whose move it was, or what the next move was.

"You may all report to your regularly scheduled classes." Suddenly, the noise level jumped at least 10 decibels as every student in the auditorium began to take their exit. That is, every student but one.

I just sat there. I wasn't sure what this meant for me. I knew it was because of me, but how was it going to impact how the other peers interacted with me?

Why don't you go ask, child? Superego cooed.

Ask what? Dumbly, I replied.

Ask Sgt. Saroka and Mr. Mitchell what it's going to mean. Superego explained. *They would know. They're the adults who are setting this ball in motion. They must have some idea of what they're trying to accomplish.*

You're right, I replied. Standing, I slowly made my way over to the podium.

This isn't going to work. You know that, right? Id retorted.

You don't know that. Superego rolled her eyes.

Like hell I don't. These bastards aren't going to stop being rude, crude, crass and immature anymore than they can control their breathing. Id kept pushing Superego's button, hoping for a battle.

You don't know that if you don't give them a chance.

What the hell have we been doing for the past decade?! I don't EVER recall getting what I want, pushing kids off swings, punching those little shits in their faces, none of that!

Violence never solved any problems. It only escalates things and makes them worse. Superego sighed. It was like arguing with a child who would never see the validity to the other side of the argument.

And what problems have we caused that they feel violence is an acceptable justification to deal with us? Exactly. We've been doing what you want. Now it's time to shut the fuck up and move over, because a new sheriff's in town! Id grinned.

That's what you think! Superego hissed back.

I kept walking. Slowly but surely, I reached the podium.

"Yes?" Mr. Mitchell asked. His monotone voice revealed a slight inflection of annoyance and anger. Was he angry with me?

"I just wanted to know what things were going to be like." I asked numbly. I wasn't sure how to phrase my concerns.

"Well, as I had mentioned, the police will be taking shifts patrolling the hallways. If there is any suspicious activity taking place, the police have full authority to deal with the matters." Mr. Mitchell gave an empty hearted smile.

I nodded in false understanding.

"Go on. Get to class." With that, my presence was dismissed. Turning around, I headed in the direction of where I was "supposed" to be.

Oh, that was helpful. Id sneered.

Maybe she should've been clearer about what she wanted to know.
Superego sneered back.

Why don't you just shut up? You have no idea what you're talking about! Id snapped.

Excuse me? I have no idea what I'm talking about? That'd be the pot calling the kettle black!

I don't fucking think so.

Oh yeah, that's right. Your answer is to use toxic chemicals and level everyone in the building!

And what's wrong with that? Id's expression was motionless. It reminded me of a panther right before it pounced.

I told you, violence doesn't solve anything. Besides, with the police roaming the hallways, the other students aren't going to do anything to us. Superego's tone decreased in an effort to maintain composure.

And I'm telling you, I don't care if the police <u>are</u> roaming the halls. 'Where there's a will, there's a way.' Isn't that what mom is always saying the biggest key to success is? 'Where there's a will, there's a way.' Id replied.

And what does that mean? Superego asked.

It means that if the other students want to hurt me, the cops won't stop

them. My heart broke at the truth.

Don't think like that, honey. I'm sure the police have the best

intentions. Superego cooed.

Maybe so, but they're not going to stop the other kids from bullying me.

I pouted, fighting back the tears.

October 22, 2006   3:13pm

So there was a surprise assembly today. Literally. It wasn't on the morning

schedule. Usually when they're going to have assemblies, they hand us a

piece of paper saying how long it is, how much shorter our other classes

are, blah blah. Not today. Whatever. It sucked anyways. I guess Mr.

Mitchell is going to have the police monitor the hallways to make sure

none of the other students are giving me crap. I'm sure mom will be

thrilled when she hears the news. I don't think it's going to work. I know

these bastards. I've went to school with them for 10 years. They wanted to

make my life a living hell, and they've succeeded. I just wish I knew why.

I never did anything to them. Why would they hurt me? I wish I knew.

Maybe if I knew why, I could reason with them and convince them it was

a bad idea. I just have no idea. I just know in my heart that they will

continue hurting me. Short of taking out the entire school, nothing will

stop them. They won't ever stop themselves. Hopefully, it doesn't come to

me stopping them. If it comes to that, they're never going to be able to do

a goddamn thing ever again!

Chapter 23

As usual, I played solitaire on my computer to pass away the afternoon hours. As usual, I won more games than I lost. However, this time was different. It was as if I was in school, stalking the clock. I anxiously awaited mom's arrival. I desperately wanted someone to talk to about it. It was not as if the phone would ring, and my bestest friend in the whole wide world would call me. The phone never rang for me. I didn't have any friends. My only friends were my computer, my mom, and me.

Glancing at the clock, it said 5:17pm. *Mom should be home any minute,* I thought to myself.

Maybe she'll have the answers you seek, Superego smiled.

Doubt it. She wasn't there today. How the hell would she know? Id frowned.

The slamming of a door downstairs interrupted their argument from going further. Without a seconds' thought, I bounded down the stairs to greet my only friend.

"Hey!" I smiled, happy to see her.

"Hey honey. How was the rest of your day at school?" Mom smiled back.

"It was weird. We had this assembly and Sgt. Saroka was there. Mr. Mitchell said that from now on, anyone caught bullying another student will deal with the police!" I gushed.

"Really?" Mom seemed slightly, but genuinely, shocked.

"Yeah." I nodded.

"It sounds as if they're serious about keeping everyone safe." Mom rummaged in the fridge.

"Yeah." My concerns echoed in my voice, and mom peeked her head out from behind the door.

"What's the matter, honey? You don't sound convinced." Mom's tone matched my concerns, although for different reasons.

"I just keep thinking about what you said. 'Where there's a will, there's a way.'" I responded sadly.

"Oh honey, I meant if you wanted to succeed in life, then nothing should stop you." Mom half smiled at me.

"I know what you meant. You meant if you are determined to do something, then nothing will stop you."

"The police will be a heck of a deterrent, don't you think?" Her eyes were hopeful, and they desperately sought reassurance.

I shrugged. I wanted to believe her, but I couldn't shake my doubts.

"Oh, come on honey. This will soon be over. I promise." Mom smiled at me, trying to spread her optimism.

I falsely smiled back, hoping to appease her.

Did you hear? She said this will all be over soon. Superego brimmed with peaceful happiness.

I know it will. The second I gas those mother fuckers, it WILL be over. Id grinned.

"So what are the plans for the rest of the night?" Mom asked.

"I don't know. What do you want to do?" I asked.

"Is there anything good on TV?" Mom thought aloud.

"I don't think so." Furrowing my brow, I tried to remember which regularly scheduled shows would be on that night.

"Well, how about we talk for a bit?"

"Okay. What's up?"

"You know the trial has begun."

"When?" I was surprised. I hadn't heard anything about it. "Last I knew, she just had charges brought against her."

"Technically, it starts tomorrow." Mom said.

"Do I have to go in?"

"You go in next Monday to testify. Other than that, you have no reason to be there. Besides, Cindy will tell me everything that happens at the end of the day." Mom smiled.

"What am I supposed to say?"

"Tell the truth. Just say what you said when we talked to Cindy. Don't lie, don't exaggerate, just tell the truth."

"Okay. Do I get to be there when she's sentenced?" I asked with a slight smile.

"Why, do you want to be?"

"Kind of."

"Why?"

"I just want to." I shrugged.

Admit it. You want to see that bitch fry! Id squealed. *Fry, bitch. Fry!*

You should take pity on her. She made a mistake. Everyone makes mistakes. Superego scowled.

Yeah. Everyone makes mistakes. Not everyone hurts people. I hissed at Superego. *Now, both of you. Shut up!*

"I suppose you can be there at the sentencing." Mom sighed, shaking her head.

"When is she going to be sentenced?"

"When the trial is over."

"And when is that?" I asked, impatient.

"I don't know. We'll have to wait and see." Bugging her eyes out, she made an exaggerated goofy stare at me.

Nodding, I had no other course of action. I had no idea what to say, and the silence slowly took over.

"So what would you like for dinner?" Mom asked, trying to drive the uninvited third party out of the conversation.

"Mashed potatoes and chicken gravy!" I squealed in excitement.

"Are you going to peel the potatoes?" She asked, squinting an eye at me.

"Are you going to make the gravy?" I replied with an ersatz squint of my own.

"Answer my question first and I'll answer yours."

I couldn't maintain composure any longer. I cracked up laughing. "Sure, mom." With a return grin on her face, I fetched the potatoes and a peeler. Sitting by the garbage can, I began to throw away the skins that the peeler stripped off of the potato like a careless harlot in a back alley.

"Thought you might like this." Mom delicately dropped a pot next to me.

"What's that for?" I asked, confused.

"To put the potatoes in when you're done peeling them." Mom answered.

Nodding, I went back to my mindless work. It was repetitive and unskilled. It may have sounded strange, but I enjoyed this line of chores. It was easy to focus on something else without screwing up, and it gave me a chance to think. Think about all the things that were happening, all of the things that pissed me off, think about the best way to handle them, and best of all, to think about the future.

How do I feel about the police monitoring the halls? I pondered, my right arm still stroking in a downward motion. *Well, if they actually maintain order, I suppose it'll be a good thing. I mean, they ARE cops. They know how to handle trouble.*

That's what they're there for, Superego smiled. I think maybe she thought I was returning to her side of the logic argument.

Yeah, and the second their backs are turned, BAM! Shit's going to hit the fan! Id retorted.

Rolling my eyes, I tried to shake my two sides away from any conscious radar. I wanted them off of my detection screen. I couldn't pick one side over the other. They both made convincing arguments.

"Alright, babe. I think that's enough potatoes." Mom took the peeler out of my hand. Drifting back to reality, I looked around. There was a mound of rinds in the garbage. *Where did they come from?* I wondered.

Walking over to the sink, I washed my hands. That was the only down side to making mashed potatoes from scratch. Your hands smelled like dirt.

"When will dinner be done?" I asked, rubbing my hands together.

"In about an hour." Mom replied.

"Okay. I'm going to go play on my computer." Turning off the faucet, I dried my hands on my pants as I bounded up the stairs and rejoined my patiently waiting confidant.

October 22, 2006 6:13pm

So, mom thinks the police being at the school from now on is a good idea. She doesn't think the kids will hurt me. I wish she would think about the POSSIBILITY that it COULD happen. She doesn't know that it won't. I don't know. We'll have to see what happens, I guess. On the bright side, the trial starts soon. And I get to testify! I hope they put that bitch away for a long time! And I get to be there when she's sentenced! Awesome! Alright, well I'm going to play solitaire until dinner's ready.

Chapter 24

Wandering around the hallways in school had never been an activity that I gave a second thought to. However, when there are police officers around every corner, it demands your attention. Students were slower getting to class. Everyone was distracted by these immobile lifeless leviathans that could strike at any moment.

With a smile, I walked into my second period gym class. Today, I got to see Justin. It was a nice reprieve, especially from the drama that happened yesterday!

Scanning the room, I looked back and forth until I saw his beautiful auburn curls. Instantly, a smile lit up my face as my feet took flight.

"Justin!" I half cried, half shouted. Looking over at me, I began to wave to him.

"Hey. Sup?" He replied with a nonchalant smile.

"Not much. Did you hear? The trial started today." I was so excited to be able to talk to someone that the words gushed out before I could censor them.

"I heard. Everyone is talking about it." He nodded.

"I get to testify."

"When?"

"Sometime next week."

"Cool."

"You want to come?" I asked, my heart pounding. I knew I could count on my mom for support. I secretly hoped that I could count on my peers as well.

"Sure. Just let me know a day in advance." He nodded.

"Cool." I smiled.

"Hey. A bunch of us are getting together and watching movies this weekend. You want to come? They'll be blood and guts, hack and thrash movies." He grinned.

"Hell yeah! Those are my favorite kind!" I grinned back.

"Awesome. I'll tell you Friday when and where." He kept grinning.

"Cool." I kept grinning.

"O'Reilly! Move it, NOW!" His teacher shrieked, obviously displeased with our repetitive get-togethers.

"See you." I waved.

"See you Friday." I waved back.

I was so happy! I had never been invited anywhere by a classmate! I never went to any of their birthday parties or holiday parties. Nothing. No one bothered to send me anything. Even when I was in elementary school, I only got Christmas and Valentine's Day cards because they were mandatory. But I never got any of the candy that the other students got.

By the beginning of third period, I was still walking on air. Nothing could bring me down! I was no longer the outsider. I was one of them, one of the "cool kids."

Taking my seat, Mrs. Grant waited patiently for the other students to arrive. I usually didn't arrive early, but today I had a bounce in my step.

The second that bell rang, Mrs. Grant's voice chirped her morning hellos. "Good morning, class." She smiled.

"Good morning." We mumbled in reply.

"Today, we are going to discuss a project that you will be working on. You will be assigned partners, and it will be due at the end of next week." She smiled.

Suddenly, the happiness that elated me not ten seconds prior had deflated. Fear took over as my stomach seized. Did she really say 'partner'?

I hate working with people! I thought grouchily. *Not really. They hate working with me.*

"When I call your names, I want you to move to your partner and sit next to them. Abby and Chris. Jen and Mark. Robin and Andrew..." She rattled off. Looking over at my 'partner', my heart sank. Andrew was one of the most popular boys in my grade. There's no way he'd want to be seen with me. I knew in my gut that because of that fact, he wouldn't put any effort into this project. Either I did all the work myself, or I failed. It depended on how she graded us.

"Okay, now find your partners." Her enthusiasm was starting to wear thin on my cranial petechiai, causing a headache. I looked over at Andrew again. He was gabbing away with his friends, making no effort to find me.

Rolling my eyes, I swung my bag over my shoulder and skulked over to him. I stood there in the shadows, not saying a word. I waited patiently for him to acknowledge me. After a couple minutes though, it was apparent that he wasn't interested.

"Shall we?" I snipped, raising my eyebrows.

He shrugged in response.

Spinning on my heels, I found the nearest available table. Silently, he sat down next to me.

"This project consists of making a children's book. You will need a theme, pictures, characters, and dialogue. You are welcome to contact your partner outside of class. However, all work must be turned in at the end of the day." She smiled.

"So what do you want to do?" I asked.

He shrugged again.

Gritting my teeth, I took a deep breath. This was going to be a difficult 8 days, judging by his level of cooperation.

"Can you draw?" I asked, trying not to let my irritation show.

"Yeah." His voice was soft, barely audible.

"So, how about this? How about I do the story line, and you draw the cartoons?" I asked.

"Sure."

"Okay." Briefly turning my attention to my bag for a piece of paper, I heard the squeak of a chair being pushed back. When I looked up, Andrew was gone.

You son of a bitch! I cursed to myself. *I swear to god, if I get a bad grade on this, I'm going to kick his ass! This is bullshit! WE are supposed to be doing this project, not ME!*

Kick his ass! Kick his ass! Id jumped up and down with excitement.

Knock it off. He's just talking to his friends. If you ask him politely, he'll come back and help you. Superego scolded.

Shaking my head, I began to brainstorm. *Fuck him,* I thought. *If I do the project by myself, then I'll tell Mrs. Grant. Then Andrew won't get any credit. That'll show him. That's fair.*

An idea hit me as soon as I thought that. What if the story line was about kids in a classroom cooperating? But the kids were animals? Like baby bunnies and kitties and puppies, and they were all sharing and caring?

That's a great title! I thought, getting excited myself. *Caring and sharing.*

Soon, I began scribbling down characters, speeches, and interactions. I was happy to be in my own little world, away from the rest of the class. Away from Andrew. I was completely unaware how much time had passed until I heard the bell. Everyone jumped up from their seats and ran out the door as I scrambled to catch up.

"Got any work to hand in?" Mrs. Grant smiled.

Extending my hand, I pushed the pages forward.

"What's the idea?" She asked.

"A classroom with animals." I replied. Hearing the condensed version made me doubt myself. Was this concept 'too cute'?

"Nice. I see the title is 'Caring and sharing'." She nodded.

"Yep."

"Looks like you and Andrew got far." She smiled again.

"Well, I did that." Oops. I didn't mean for her to find out so soon that he was incompetent and neglectful!

"Oh? And what did Andrew do all period?" She asked, her eyebrows furrowing. She was obviously displeased with the news.

"I don't know. I know he went to talk to his friends, but I don't know who." I shrugged, trying to end this conversation quickly.

"Okay. You'd better get to your next class. I'll see you tomorrow."

Without a moment's notice, I flew out the door. Her words didn't stay in my head. Her tone, however, did. She was irate!

Sighing, I jogged to my next class. It seemed like trouble followed me no matter where I went. Even if I wasn't trying to start any, it found me.

My good mood was permanently ruined the rest of the day.

October 23, 2006 2:45 pm

Damn it! I have a project to do in English! The worst part is that I have a

partner! Is name is Andrew, and he's a total jackass! I'm busting my ass

working on the project, while he's socializing with his friends! What a

fucking cock! Oh well. I told Mrs. Grant. She's going to deal with him

tomorrow, I guess. His problem, not mine. I've <u>been</u> doing my work! Oh, I

almost forgot! I guess this Friday I'm going to hang out and watch movies

with Justin! He invited me! Isn't that so cool?

Chapter 25

I had no desire to go to school the next day. I knew that Mrs. Grant

would talk to Andrew, and I knew that Andrew would be pissed off at me.

Regardless of the circumstances, I knew Andrew was going to blame me

for his actions. I knew that's how it would be.

Oh well, I thought. *No use running from trouble. It always finds me.*

Might as well get this over with.

Trudging through the halls, I veered towards the cafeteria. Today, I was

blessed with two glorious study halls. Having no tangible homework

meant I could sleep.

That's retarded, I griped. *They should've let me stay home and slept in*

the first two periods. They let the seniors do that. Why is attendance

mandatory for freshmen? Shaking my head, I meandered over to my seat

while in accordance with yet another arbitrary rule.

Ignoring any and all outside stimuli, I buried my attention into my book

bag and closed my eyes. As the world carried on around me, I tried to process everything that had happened, and everything I believed would happen.

Okay, well Andrew and I still have to finish that project... I began. *And Mrs. Grant is going to 'talk to him' about not helping me yesterday. What if he gets angry?*

It's normal for people to get angry when they get chastised. Superego cooed. *Just let him hang out with his friends, and only ask him for his help when it's absolutely necessary.*

Meanwhile, the little fuck gets a free pass to 'Do whatever the fuck you want' town, and you expect her to be okay with it? Bullshit! Get off your fat, lazy, worthless ass and work! Id fumed.

Taking in a deep breath, I had to agree with the latter. It wasn't fair for me to put in all the work and for him to piggy back off of my labors. If he wanted to get any kind of a non-failing grade, he should have to earn it like the rest of us.

Maybe this world would be a little nicer if we all showed a little more compassion to each other. Superego scoffed.

Maybe, but that's not how the real world works. In the REAL world, everyone is a selfish asshole who hasn't done anything noteworthy or worth living for. Everyone is so self absorbed, that they can't see what the fuck is happening, if it does pertain to them. Id hissed back.

That's not true. Everyone lives very busy lives. They're just trying to make the best of it. Superego shook her head.

Bullshit! When she got slammed into that locker, what the fuck did those bitches in the bathroom do? Absolutely nothing! They didn't even fucking ask if she was okay! Is it that hard to ask someone if they're okay? I don't fucking think so! They didn't ask because they don't care! Id screeched. *I say we bomb the hell out of everyone, and anyone who survives, make them behave better or bomb them again!*

Flipping my head over, I nestled my right cheek against my bag. It broke my heart to be so divided. I wanted to believe the best in people, but no one showed that side. How was one to see what being a good person looked like if all around you was narcissistic and destructive behavior?

Taking in another deep breath, I tried to focus my attentions on another topic.

Justin invited me to hang out and watch movies. I smiled.

Isn't that sweet? You have a friend! Superego returned the smile.

I wouldn't trust the bastard. I'm sure he doesn't give a damn about you. He's only doing it because it serves one of his needs. Id grumbled.

And what need is that? Superego challenged.

I don't fucking know! I'm just saying, nobody has bothered to talk to her or try to be her friend before. Why now? What the hell has changed to make the outcome any different? Id continued to grumble.

My stomach seized. I knew that Id had a valid point. If I was such a good person and so easy to get along with, then why hasn't anyone tried to be my friend before now? Why has everyone in school harassed me, rather than be nice to me?

Shaking my head slightly, I brushed off my worries. *No,* I thought. *I actually have a friend, and I am going to enjoy 'hanging out' with people. It's not a big deal. We're just going to watch movies.*

With the world continuing to rotate on its axis, I listened to the mundane chatter going on around me. None of it was of any importance, but somehow, it made me feel more connected to my peers. Just knowing what they valued as important, and that I knew a part of their lives, made a difference in mine. Not that they cared. Not that they'd tell me to my face. Oh well. Second hand knowledge was better than none, I supposed.

When the bell rang, I looked up at the clock. Bewildered, I roused from my chair. It was already time for me to go to third period. *What happened to the bell in between first and second period? I must've spaced out and not even heard it!*

My heart began to pound as I trudged towards my destiny. Even though they clutched the straps of my bag, I could feel my hands trying to thrash against their restraints.

I shouldn't be nervous. I didn't do anything wrong. I tried to reassure myself, but to no avail. It was an exercise in futility.

Taking my seat, I scanned the room. I didn't see Andrew anywhere, but Mrs. Grant smiled at me. I offered an empty smile back. I couldn't muster the enthusiasm to offer a real one.

"Okay, class. I looked over the work everyone handed back, and overall, I'm pleased with what I saw. Today, you're going to get with your partners and continue work. On Friday, I will meet with each of you individually to make sure you're on track." She smiled. "Now, please go sit with your partner while I hand back your preliminary work."

I took in a deep breath and held it. What if she confronted Andrew about his non participation when she met with us on Friday? Then he'd know I said something!

Watching all of my peers move about made me more and more nervous. Where was Andrew?

When Mrs. Grant handed me back my work, she was thinking the same thing. "Where's your partner?" She asked.

I shrugged. "I don't know."

"Well, who's your partner?" She asked another question.

"Andrew." I replied. Looking around, I spotted him talking to his friends. Rolling my eyes quickly, I pointed to him. "He's right there."

"Well, why isn't he with you working on your project?" She began to sound slightly irate.

I shrugged. I didn't have any answer to give her.

Dropping her papers on my desk, she spun on her heels and walked over to Andrew. Leaning over, she whispered something in his ear. I couldn't make out what she said. When she stood up, Andrew stood up

with her. Then the two of them went into the hallways.

Everyone looked around. We were all confused. Nobody knew what

was going on. At least I had an advantage. I had an inkling what was

going on. He was getting in trouble, because of me.

It's not because of anything you did. He brought it on himself.

Superego tried to calm my frazzled nerves.

I still feel bad, I thought.

Do you think he 'feels bad' that you're doing all the work? Fuck, no he

doesn't! Id snapped.

The chatter around me immediately died down when they returned.

Mrs. Grant looked slightly annoyed, but Andrew... he was a mix between

upset and angry.

I hope he isn't angry with me, I thought.

He should be angry with himself. Superego stated.

With his head down, he walked over to my desk. Without saying a

word, he dropped into the seat next to me.

That's right, asshole. Keep your head down. Don't fucking look at me. Id challenged.

Mrs. Grant walked over to my desk and rescued us from baby sitting her papers. "You may begin working on your projects." Mrs. Grant smiled as she continued passing them out.

Quickly, I looked at Andrew. His head was still down. He was lost in his own little world. Shrugging to myself, I began working on our assignment.

Every few minutes, I would steal a glance at Andrew. I felt guilty and sad, like I was responsible for him getting in trouble, and now he was mad at me. He didn't have to say anything. I just knew.

As the depression waves moved to high tide, my heart broke a little bit more.

There is no way I'm going to make it through high school, I thought. As soon as third period was over, I made my way out the side door. I was too depressed to sit through any more of my classes. I knew I was going to get in trouble. I didn't care. I couldn't be confined by their hatred and disapproval any longer. So I walked along the highway home, taking the path I was becoming well acquainted with.

When I had arrived to my sanctum sanctorum, I bounded up the stairs and crawled in bed with the hopes of taking a nap. I desperately wanted to escape reality.

I lay in bed and listened to the silence. Try as I might, I couldn't fall asleep. My mind was racing with dozens of thoughts. I couldn't isolate any of them to analyze a single one. So I listened to the silence. I knew it would be quiet. No one ever called for me. My mother would have, but she did not know I had gone home.

I guess that's one of the perks of having no friends, I considered. *If I cherished silence, then I would be in heaven!*

It broke my heart to be so alone. I ached for companionship, for any companionship. Even if it were a dog or a cat, I would've been so happy. To have some living thing that enjoyed my company.

The seconds dragged by. The only things I could hear was the clock in the hallway ticking by the loneliness, and the sounds of my soul dying for a chance to be "normal."

October 24, 2006   12:46 pm

I couldn't take it. I had to come home at lunch again. Mom's going to be
pissed at me. Oh well. I don't care anymore. Andrew got upset with me
today. I knew he wasn't going to help me with our damn project. So when
he got in trouble, he got mad at me! That's fucking crap! I couldn't be in
that place anymore. I hate it, more and more every day. I can't stand it!
Everything I do is wrong. Everyone always gets mad at me, even if they're
the ones fucking up! I'm sick of it! I'm sick of getting crap, I'm sick of
their bullshit, and I'm sick of the adults thinking that they're 'helping'.
They're not fucking helping! They're only making things worse!! Well,
I'm going to play solitaire.

Chapter 26

As the minutes passed by, I waited for my little blue piece of paper to find me. I knew it would. I had left school right before lunch the previous school day. Regardless of my reasons for doing so, the adults didn't care. They disapproved, and their word was law.

When it floated down to me, my emotions were a roller coaster of extremes. First, I was angry. How could they punish me?! Then I was scared. I didn't want to get in trouble! Last, I was sad. I knew this would mean that I would get detention. Wonderful.

This time, I was numb walking to the main office. The police officer's presence standing in the hallway barely registered as I followed the path of destiny. It was almost like I knew that I was getting detention, and I didn't care. I had already accepted it, and moved on.

"Ms. Edwards?" Mr. Mitchell called from his office. Standing up, I followed his unspoken command of "come". When I had sat down, he looked up at me from my ever growing folder on his desk.

"It seems you were here for your first three classes, and then we have no record of your attendance." He began in his usual tone. It was enough to put anyone to sleep.

I remained silent in my chair, unsure of what to say.

"Did something happen yesterday?" He asked, desperately seeking to withdraw information from me.

Yes, mother fucker. Another one of your precious students pissed her off yesterday! What the fuck did the cops do? Absolutely nothing! Id shrieked.

I shrugged.

"What happened? I can't help if you don't tell me." He smiled a hollow "I'm an adult and I'll make it all better for the little child" smile.

I wanted to scream at him. The mire of the situation was apparent only to me. Nobody understood what was happening! It was enough to drive a mad man sane!

"There's this guy in my English class…" I began. Pausing, I wasn't sure what to say next.

"Oh, and you like him." Mr. Mitchell smiled again.

"No." I crinkled my face, my nostrils flaring in disgust and loathe at the wretchedness of the idea of Andrew. "We have a project to do in English class, and he won't help me."

"Did you talk to your teacher about it?" He leaned into the conversation.

"Yeah, and she talked to Andrew." I replied.

"Then, what's the problem?" He asked, furrowing his brows.

"Andrew's mad at me." I pouted slightly.

"Did he do something?"

"No."

"Then how do you know he's mad at you?"

"He won't talk to me."

"Well, this sounds like an issue to take up with your teacher." He leaned back in his chair. "Meanwhile, you cannot be skipping classes. I'm going to have to give you one day of In School Suspension for missing the rest of your classes. You can report to ISS on Monday morning."

ISS? My head screamed. *NOOOO!* That meant I'd have to spend an entire day with Mr. Fout. My stomach turned at the realization of what that day would entail.

"Run along to your first period class." Looking down, I had lost his attention, leaving no room to negotiate. The conversation was over.

Dragging myself out of his office, I hung my head low as I walked over to the secretary.

"Can I have a hall pass, please?" I mumbled, heartbreak resonating in my voice.

"Sure dear. Where are you headed to?" She smiled.

"Study hall in the cafeteria."

Quickly, she scribbled down the time and place and handed me the slip. Smiling once again, I fared an ersatz smile and disappeared into the hallway.

I was in no hurry to reach my destination. It was study hall, and not having anything to distract me was going to be crushingly horrendous. I knew all I was going to think about was an entire day with Mr. Fout. I didn't want to see him, or hear his smug, cocky attitude about what kind of sandwich I was given for lunch. I knew he would delight in dictating my every move for an entire 6 hours! It was unbearable!

As I curled up against my book bag, a shattering realization occurred to me. At least I wasn't going to miss gym. I was going to get to talk to Justin! Breathing a sigh of relief, I knew I had temporarily found a distraction from next Monday's impending agony.

Laying my head down, I began to think of all of the possibilities. What kind of movies were we going to watch? Who all was going to be there? What if it was just me and Justin?

Impatiently, I looked at the clock. I desperately wanted to hear the bell. *Come on!* I whined. *Ring already!*

What felt like 10 minutes (and most likely was) passed before the bell complied with my demands. Jumping out of my seat, I rushed to my next class.

Searching the room with my skillful achromatic sense, I desperately sought Justin. No sign of him.

You are a little earlier than usual dear. Just be patient. I'm sure he'll arrive momentarily. Superego cooed.

Bullshit. He knows he's supposed to tell you what's going on, and he's not going to show up. He doesn't give a damn about you. Kick his ass! Id avenged.

Resuming my search, I decided to include my peripheral scope. Hopefully, he would appear on my visual radar. Still, I saw no sign of that beautiful curly hair.

"Okay, class. Let's get started." My teacher called.

Panic resonated my entire nervous system as I realized I hadn't found Justin, and class had begun. Hanging my head once again, I turned slowly and joined my peers. I stopped within 5 feet of the two hyenas who considered me a "snitch" and stared off into space. The teacher continued her instructions regarding today's activity, oblivious at our lack of enthusiasm.

Blowing her whistle quickly snapped me back to reality. Unfortunately, I had no idea what was going on. Looking to my peers, I tried to quickly read their body language for a clue.

"Is there a problem, Robin?" Mrs. Roki asked.

"No." I shook my head quickly, moving towards the girls. Jogging to catch up, their chatter screeched to a halt as I approached their bubble.

"What do you want, freak?" The girl who called me a snitch asked.

"Nothing." I barely spoke above a whisper, my face hung low with sorrow.

"Then, why are you here?" She snipped.

I shrugged. "I don't know what we're doing."

"We're supposed to find something to do." She darted her head forward, emphasizing her desire for me to disappear.

"Oh. Okay, thanks." Turning around, I looked for a ball. There weren't many left. All I needed was one kickball...

Finally, I got up the courage to ask the guys. Walking over I asked, "Is there a kickball anywhere?"

Without making eye contact, "Over there. By the bleachers." A voice floated over to me.

Following their directions, I picked up a ball. I dropped it on the floor and began nudging it with my foot. My new companion and I played cat and mouse for the next half an hour without disturbance. Sadly, I would

occasionally glance up in search for Justin. Still, no sign of him.

"Okay everyone. Have a nice weekend." Mrs. Roki's whistle shrieked

at us. "Put the equipment away and you're free to go."

Nudging the ball with my foot, I sulked over to the bleachers to return

the red orb of athletics. When it was near enough (at least by my

standards), I turned and walked into the locker room to change. I wanted

to be as far away from gym class as I could, as fast as I could.

This is fucking wonderful, I grumbled. *First, that fat fuck gives me*

detention. Second of all, Justin blew me off. This is going to be a

wonderful weekend.

I told you that mother fucker didn't give a crap about you. Id sneered.

Shut up! Can't you tell she's hurting? Shame on you for delighting in

her misery! Superego scolded.

I don't care! I warned her about these assholes. I told her they didn't

care and that she shouldn't open up to them. If she did, she was only going

to get hurt. Maybe instead of thinking everyone is so sweet and wonderful,

she should learn that everyone sucks and that in the end, she can only count on herself. Id retorted. *Maybe she'll listen to me now when I tell her to gas these bastards. They don't care about her, so why should she care about them?*

The loneliness of playing solitaire for yet another weekend was very depressing. With every step, the pain of rejection and solitude strangled any hope of obtaining a different reality.

I just sat in Mrs. Grant's class, begging to be left alone with my misery. I didn't want to deal with Andrew just sitting there being a schmuck. If he didn't want to be seen associating with me, fine. Then he could be as far away from me as the classroom walls would allow. I was going to be miserable with or without his presence. It made no difference to me what his actions were. However, to have him near me would mean I would have to face the possibility that another realm of emotion existed; that I could be happy just like my peers. But happiness was something I would never be able to obtain. I would never have friends. I would never share an inside joke with anyone. I would always be isolated and alone.

Unable to focus on the project, I kept reading and rereading the progress I had made. The words took on the shapes of unfamiliar squiggles as my eyes failed to relay their message. The hollow emptiness inside my heart resonated, distracting me from accomplishing any work.

As the seconds passed by, everything began taking on a blurry unrecognizable form. Nothing seemed familiar. Nothing made sense. As seconds turned into minutes, and minutes turned into hours, I allowed habit to take over and guide me through the rest of the day. Whatever part of my personality that I usually incorporated into my daily rituals had faded, choosing to hide from the cruel reality that was high school.

October 25, 2006   2:57pm

Today was just fucking awesome! First, I got detention for missing my

classes yesterday! Mr. Mitchell didn't care why. So I have to spend all day

Monday with Mr. Fout. That's fucking crap! I hate him! He's so mean to

everyone! He acts like he owns the room! Um, no dude! You're just the

detention teacher! You aren't king of the school! Prick! Then, Justin didn't

show up to gym class! We were supposed to get together tonight to watch

movies! So now I just get to stay home alone by myself all weekend (as

usual) and play solitaire. Then I saw Andrew. That bastard didn't help

with the project at all again, and it's due next week. He could be fucking

drawing the frames for the story, but no! He's got to talk to his friends!

Because that's more important! I hate high school! I can't wait for it to be

over!! I don't want to wait 3 ½ more years! I want it over with NOW!

Chapter 27

"Click, click, click…" The same repetitious sound echoed through the entire upstairs. To anyone cognitive in the technological age, it was the sound of a mouse being fired in rapid succession as the cards of the computer game moved in accordance. It was the only sound to be heard. The sound of squealing girly laughter was absent as the phone remained on the base. There were no screams coming from the DVD player (as promised). No horror movies. No friends. Nobody. Just me and the computer, passing the hours and the days until my presence was mandatory in detention.

An ever growing creak-thump could be heard. There were 13 of them to be exact, as the floorboards shifted under an outside weight. A "rap, rap, rap" introduced a new sound and a new method to pass the time.

"Knock, knock kiddo." Mom said as she opened the door to my haven.

"Sup?" I asked in a monotone tone of my own.

"I just wanted to see what you were doing." She came and sat down on the bed.

"Just playing solitaire." A hollow response was uttered. I continued with my repetitive click of the mouse.

"You've been up here all weekend. Tell me that is not all you've been doing!" Mom asked incredulously.

"Okay, then I won't tell you." I laughed.

"Oh, honey! You cannot be a hermit! You have to get out and live a little!" Mom joined in the laughter.

"I'm not aspiring to be a hermit. I just like playing solitaire." I shrugged.

"So talk to me. What's up? What's happening? What's going on?" Mom nudged me with her shoulders like we were girlfriends about to gossip.

"Nothing. Sup with you?" I responded.

"Oh, come on. Something has to be up. Talk to me." Mom grinned.

Sighing, I mumbled, "Well, I have detention tomorrow."

"Why?!" Her grin was replaced with exasperation by the news.

"Stupid shit."

"Watch your language! And that doesn't tell me why."

Turning around in my computer chair, I looked her straight in the eye. She seemed instantaneously tired, as if the insurmountable stress of having a teenager was catching up to her.

"What?" I snapped. I didn't mean to allow my words to have a bite to them. I was just tired of complaining about the conditions of high school and my peers to anyone and everyone, and NO one would listen!

"Why do you have detention?" She asked, matching my bite with one from her own collection.

"Because I went home on Thursday."

"And why did you do that?" She pressed.

"Because."

"Because why?"

"It's a long story." I sighed.

Crossing her arms, Mom wiggled her derriere in the comforter. "I have time. I'm listening."

Taking in a deep breath, I closed my eyes. I knew my words weren't going to come out right, and I knew nobody would understand my rationale. That is, nobody but myself.

"Well, I'm supposed to do a project to do in class for English…" I began.

"Don't tell me you skipped school because you didn't want to do your project!" Mom scolded.

"No, I'm not saying that. If you'd listen, you know. Please don't interrupt." It was my turn to scold her for bad manners. Over the years, she had consistently corrected my bad behavior. Turn about is fair play.

"Like I was saying, I have a project to do in class for English. I have a partner. His name is Andrew, except he isn't doing anything! Everyday, he just goes and hangs out with his friends while I'm doing all the work…"

"Did you talk to the teacher about this?" Mom asked.

"Geez! You're starting to sound like Mr. Mitchell! Yes, I fucking talked to Mrs. Grant about it! You'd know that if you shut up and listened to me!" I shrieked.

"Watch your language." Mom spoke barely above a whisper.

"I'm sorry. It's pissing me off that you keep interrupting. You want to know what's going on, then shut up and listen. I'm trying to tell you!" I snapped.

"Like I was <u>trying</u> to say for the second time before I was so <u>rudely</u> interrupted for a second time," I began again. "I <u>did</u> talk to Mrs. Grant about it. The next day, she dragged Andrew out in the hallway in front of everyone! Then he just sat down next to me. He didn't say a word, he didn't help me with our project. Nothing. He didn't do anything!" Closing my mouth, I stared at her.

"I don't think I understand." Mom said with a slightly puzzled look.

"I didn't get him in trouble. He did. He isn't doing a damn thing on this project! He has no right to get mad at me! And yet, it's okay if he does! And I can't get a new partner! Mrs. Grant won't do that! She's given us three days to work on this project!" I whined.

"Well, skipping school isn't the answer." Mom gently chided.

"I know it's not. But I can't deal with everyone being mad at me all the time for stupid shit!" I snapped. I was close to tears. I could feel them rising to the surface. I silently begged them to go away, but they had their own plans.

"Oh honey, don't cry." Standing up, Mom walked over to me and rubbed my shoulder. "There has to be a solution. Come sit with me on the bed and let's talk about this." Trudging over, we both sat down.

"What is it you would like?" Mom asked, still rubbing.

"I want to be left alone. I'm tired of being blamed for everything. I'm tired of being picked on. I'm tired of everyone getting mad at me for things they do. If they mess up, they have to pay the consequences, not me. But they act like it's my fault! They say the worst things possible! And I'm so <u>sick</u> of Mr. Mitchell acting like it's all in my head!" I started to cry.

"Awww, my poor baby." Mom cooed, wrapping her arms around my head in a motherly embrace. "There isn't that much left of school. I know high school just started, but there isn't that much left of school. I mean, you will attend college. But you've gotten through elementary and middle school. You can get through the rest of high school, right?"

Hearing those words broke my heart all over again. Not only was I alone at school, but now I felt like I couldn't turn to the one person who had always been there in the past for me.

"Mom! I don't want to 'get through' the rest of high school! I want to go to a different school!" I blurted out. I didn't even know where that idea came from. I had never consciously thought about it.

"Honey, I'm sure it's not that bad." Mom started petting my hair, making me sleepy.

"What happened last year when I graduated middle school?" I snipped.

"We went out to eat and had a nice dinner." Mom smiled.

"And what happened over the summer at my birthday party?" I snipped again.

"I thought you had a nice birthday. I bought you a computer." Mom frowned. I got the feeling that she thought I was disappointed.

"That's my point. I didn't HAVE a graduation party. Family sent cards, but I didn't have a party. And I didn't have a birthday party. It was just you and me. You gave me a card that said, 'Happy Birthday.' I don't have any friends! Everyone hates me! It doesn't matter what I do! They all hate me!" I continued crying with an additional sob or two.

Simultaneously, two flashbacks sprung forth from my subconscious, each laying claim to the rights of being recalled first.

I vividly remembered my 7th birthday. I had sent invitations to my entire second grade class. Since my birthday was in the summer, I anxiously awaited all year to enjoy a birthday party with my peers.

The day of the party, I was ready to go hours before the arrival of any guests. It didn't matter to me. I sat and impeccantly waited by the door.

"What are you doing?" Mom laughed. "They'll be here when the clock says noon."

"I know, Mommy." I smiled up at her, proudly wearing a birthday hat. She smiled back and wandered off into the kitchen to finish setting up.

Despite my age, I was incredibly patient. I may have been stalking the door, but I wasn't stalking the clock. I was completely unaware that hour after hour, minute after minute, crept by without anyone's presence. What made me aware of the time was Mom walking back through the living room.

"Oh my goodness! Are you still waiting?" Her face seemed sad, hidden by a mask of years of knowledge that I was unable to translate.

"Yeah." I sighed. My birthday wish, more than anything, was for my guests to start arriving. It was to have a real party, with real friends.

"Come on, honey. Let's go shopping." Mom wrapped her arms around me, helping me to my feet.

Passing the clock, I understood why Mom was leading me away from the front door. It was 5pm. Nobody had arrived, and in my heart, I knew they had no intention of coming.

Six months later, right before Christmas break, I curled up in my chair and waited for class to begin. I could hear the other students buzzing about a party they had all went to. I wasn't included in the conversation, so I had tried not to eavesdrop too much. Despite my best efforts to mind my manners, I got the full picture.

"I can't believe her mom got her a make your own ice cream sundae bar!" One boy squealed in delight.

"I know! Wasn't it awesome?!" Another girl grinned. Shamelessly, their banter continued back and forth.

"Man, Sarah's mom is the coolest!" They all cooed in unison.

That's when it hit me. Everyone had went to this birthday party. Everyone had been invited. Everyone, except for me.

I knew exactly who everyone was referring to. There was only one girl named Sarah in our class. Her name was Sarah Zimmerman. When everyone else was outwardly nasty to me, she had always been mildly pleasant. Until now.

"Hi." She smiled at me as she took her seat.

"Happy Birthday." I mumbled icily, staring at her with unblinking eyes. She furrowed her brows at me, but she didn't seem too concerned that I was upset.

I could feel the scar tearing across my soul as her body warmed the seat next to me. It was a searing sensation that ripped through my body at lightning speeds.

It was one thing when nobody showed up to your party. You could at least rationalize it and say to yourself, *Hey. Maybe they were all busy.* But when they went out of their way to avoid having you, there's no way around that. They had deliberately made it so that I hadn't come. They purposely excluded me because they didn't want me.

Mom sighed. She was at a loss for words.

"I don't know what to tell you, sweetheart." Mom finally spoke. She continued petting my hair, hoping that I would calm myself down. She petted and petted for hours, until the weekend faded off behind the horizon.

October 27, 2006 8:43 pm

Mom doesn't get it! I told her I had detention, and I told her why. I admitted what I did, but she doesn't understand why I left school. I can't stand everyone being mad at me all the time! I don't do anything to them! Why can't they just leave me alone?! I am getting so sick of everything acting like high school is so easy! It's not! It might be easy if you have friends and you're popular, but I'm not! It's hard! It's hard to go every day and deal with that shit! I don't care what anyone says! At this rate, I'm not going to make it to college!

Chapter 28

"Beep. Beep. Beep." My alarm screamed at me for attention. Groaning, I rolled over and hit the snooze button. I had no intentions of going back to sleep. I just wanted to make the noise stop.

Lying in bed, I wrestled with coming to terms with detention. I still hadn't made peace with that fact, but it was unavoidable.

Slowly peeling the covers back, I picked up my bathrobe off the floor. It was easier than getting dressed, and it provided less exposure to the drastic difference in temperature the room and the covers offered.

In a state of suspended consciousness, I numbly walked to the mirror in the bathroom. My eyes were bloodshot, screaming to the world that I was not a willing participant of the cognitive world.

I managed to get through the rest of my morning routine with little resistance. Once my body had adjusted from sleep mode to a working one, I began to pick up momentum.

Sighing, there was nothing left for me to do but face detention. I

followed the beautiful aroma produced by the delicious demitasse coming

from the kitchen.

With a slight smile, I retrieved a coffee mug out of the cabinet and

poured myself a cup of happiness.

"Good morning." Mom chirped, following my example.

"Good morning." I echoed.

"Feeling better?" Mom took a sip.

I shrugged. "Can you take me to school?"

"Sure. We're going to have to leave soon." Mom turned around to

dulcify her coffee.

"I'm ready now."

"Do you have your books and everything?" She asked, stirring.

"Everything's at school."

"Okay. Go wait in the car. I'll be right there."

Buckling the seat belt, I exhaled. I desperately wished there was a

loophole, a way to avoid spending the entire day with Mr. Fout. But alas, there wasn't. According to Mr. Mitchell, I had committed an egregious offense, and there was a price to pay.

That was a good idea for an alternative. Transferring to another high school instead of using chlorine gas. Superego whispered in my left ear.

What's wrong with my idea? Id furrowed her brows. *I think it'll teach those bastards a lesson!*

Violence will not solve all of the world's problems. Most of the time, it'll make things worse. Superego retorted.

And it's okay that they castigate her? I don't think so! Maybe if they knew how it felt, they wouldn't be so quick to do it. Id grumbled in my right ear.

It would be better to walk away. Superego countered. *There's no need to stoop to their level.*

The slam of the door brought me back to the world, making me aware that mom had entered the car. Reaching to my chest, I reaffirmed the existence of the seat belt strap.

"So, kiddo. Have you thought about what you want to do for Halloween? It's on Thursday." Mom said with a smile.

"Not really. Why? What do you want to do?" I shrugged.

"Well, we need to buy candy for trick or treaters. And I didn't know if you were going to dress up for school…" Her thoughts trailed off, as if Monday morning brain fog had disturbed the clarity of her idiom.

"I hadn't thought about it."

"Well, think about it and let me know. Okay, honey. Have a good day at school." Mom scratched my head and smiled at me as the car slowed to a stop outside the gates of hell.

"Yeah. It'll be a blast." I rolled my eyes.

"Then stop skipping classes, and you won't get detention!" Mom quipped back, still smiling. I just rolled my eyes again. Without looking back, I kept walking towards my destiny. I could hear the engine start to whine as her foot caressed the accelerator.

Seeing my peers in clusters amongst the hallways made me remember the loneliness that had plagued me on Friday. *Awesome,* I thought. *Let's see how much of an outcast I can be today.*

Walking into Mr. Fout's dungeon, I took a seat in the back corner.

"Good morning, Robin." A vindictive smile tugged at the corners of his mouth.

"Morning." I replied. It wasn't a salutation. It was more of a verification of the time.

"Looks like you'll be here all day."

"Yep."

"You know the rules. Same as lunch time, but all day long." Flicking the wrinkles out of his crossword puzzle, his eyes scrolled down to resume his progress.

Those words kept playing in my head. *All day long.* This was going to be torture! I didn't know how I was going to make it through, but I knew I needed something to distract me.

I wish I had that stupid English project to work on. I grumbled to myself. *With or without that shit-head, I'd do it.*

You are the one who put in the work, dear. Why don't you try to remember what progress you made and see if you can go from there? Superego flashed an encouraging, yet hollow, smile.

Fuck that. Why don't we finish that bullshit you started earlier? Id

challenged. *Trying to tell me that I have no good ideas! That's bullshit!*

I'm only thinking of her!

That may be true, but you have to view things in a positive manner.

What the fuck is so damn 'positive' about being in detention?! You are

so fucking stupid! You don't know what you're talking about! Just shut the

hell up! Listen to me, kid. You know you want to show these bastards

what's what. You know you want them to leave you alone, and you want to

tell them why. Just hook chlorine gas up to the air conditioning unit

outside, then lock the doors. The gas will travel through the whole school,

and nobody will be able to get out! They'll all die! Id burst into an evil

laughter.

You can't do that! Think of how many innocent people will be hurt!

Superego was mortified.

How innocent can they be? Just because they're not giving her crap,

doesn't make them innocent.

How does that make them guilty? Superego challenged.

They can see this shit happening. And what are they doing to stand up for her? Nothing. What are they doing to stop it? Nothing. They act like it's not their problem. Id answered.

Maybe they have their own problems to deal with, and she isn't doing anything to help them. Did you ever think about that?

Nope. Don't care.

Sighing, I reached in my purse to pull out a pen. If I had to endure 6 hours with the troll and his incessant crossword puzzles, then I should do my best to distract myself.

Feeling around, I recognized certain items. My fingers brushed over a hard oval shape, and I knew it was my eyeglasses case. Then I came in contact with a thicker, square block. That would be my wallet. The last item beguiled me. It was small, barely the length of my fingers. It was smoother than the wallet and the eyeglasses case.

Furrowing my brows in confusion, I encased the small foreign entity and brought its mystery to the surface for viewing purposes.

It's the cell phone your mom gave you for emergency purposes. My eyes reported back to me. Flipping it open, the screen remained blank. I randomly began pushing buttons to entice a response. No reaction.

"Robin Edwards! No cell phones allowed!" Mr. Fout screamed at me.

"Huh?" I asked, looking around.

"There are no cell phones allowed during regular class hours! Go see Mr. Mitchell! I'm sure he'd love to know what games you're trying to play."

With a sigh, I hung my head down low and began my trudge to Mr. Mitchell's office. I didn't know what was going to transpire, but I knew I would get in more trouble.

"Good morning, dear." The secretary smiled at me.

"Morning." I grumbled. It wasn't turning out to be very "good" for me.

"In my office. NOW." Mr. Mitchell snapped.

Sighing, I complied. *Let's get this shit over with.* I thought.

"What is this I hear?" Mr. Mitchell fumed as soon as the door was closed. "Mr. Fout said you had a cell phone in detention!"

I didn't reply.

"Cell phones are not allowed in classes! Students are only allowed to use them during their lunch hours!" His breathing became more rapid.

My stoic response remained in tact.

"Do you care to explain yourself, or are you just going to sit there?" He continued to fume.

"I was looking for a pen so that I could work on my English project. I forgot my mom gave it to me in case of an emergency! But it doesn't work." I protested.

"You're mother <u>gave</u> you a phone in case of an emergency? When?" He asked. His voice regained some composure.

"Uh, a couple weeks ago?" Scanning my memory banks, I tried to remember when she had given it to me.

"And since then, you could have called your mother for help. But you chose to continually skip classes rather than ask anyone for assistance."

Fuck! Id sighed. *This son of a bitch is going to nail you to the wall because of this shit. Just you watch.*

Explain to him that you forgot it was even in there. I'm sure he'll understand. Superego replied.

"I forgot she gave it to me!" I said, my eyes getting big.

"I highly doubt that a teenager would forget that their parents bought them a cell phone. I don't like being lied to, and I don't like people playing games. Due to this new insight, I'm going to assign you detention for the rest of this week." Delightfully, he began scribbling on a blue pad of paper.

"Why?" I whined.

"You could have asked me for help, or called your mother. But since you want to continue skipping school, then you lied to me about being in peril. For that, I'm assigning you In School Suspension for the entire week. I'm also assigning you detention for using a cell phone during non lunch hours." He kept scribbling.

I sighed under my breath.

Fucking asshole. Id hissed. *Still think he'll understand if you 'explain to him'?*

"You may return to Mr. Fout now." A smile graced his face as misery encompassed mine.

Upon my return, I picked up my purse. I wasn't about to keep digging around for my pen. This time, I was going to look. I dropped my cell phone back in and found what was I was looking for.

October 28, 2006 9:03am

Fuck this shit! I just got an entire week of ISS for bullshit! I told Mr.

Mitchell that I forgot my mom had even given me a phone! He doesn't

fucking care! He just thinks that I was trying to call someone during

detention. It's not true, but that's what he thinks! He doesn't fucking care!

Nobody fucking cares! They're all so quick to condemn me! That's all

they care about! I can't do anything right! Fuck this shit! I am NOT

putting up with it forever! I swear, if ONE MORE THING goes wrong

this week, I'm going to fucking snap! I'm tired of being the black sheep!

I'm sick of this shit!!

Chapter 29

I was unable to rejoice in the safety that my home brought me. How could I relax when I knew there was nothing to look forward to? I wasn't going to be able to see Justin all week, and now Mr. Mitchell viewed me as a lying manipulative teenager. My only saving grace was my mother.

Picking up the phone, I decided to call her. I couldn't wait for her to come home to discuss this. I lacked that kind of patience.

After two rings, her warm voice caressed my tattered soul.

"Hello?" She manually responded.

"Hi, mom." I replied with a smile. Immediately I began to feel comforted, just by hearing her say, "hello."

"What's up, dear? How was your day at school?" She asked.

"Horrible!" I cried. "Mr. Mitchell gave me In School Suspension all week!"

"Why? What happened?" An incredulous outcry burst from her lips.

"I was in detention today and I was looking for a pen. I found the cell phone you gave me a while ago, but it's broken. Mr. Fout thinks I was trying to call someone when I wasn't! And Mr. Mitchell doesn't care!

He's mad at me because I kept walking home instead of calling you!" My

voice kept climbing the notes on a scale, increasing in decibel levels.

"Were you trying to call me?" She asked.

"No. The stupid thing's broken. I tried pushing buttons, but the screen

stayed black." I responded.

"Did you charge it?"

"What?"

"Well, if you didn't charge it, then the battery most likely died."

"So, where do we keep the spare batteries?" I asked, going to the

garage.

"No, no, no dear. Cell phone batteries can be recharged. You don't

have to replace them like the batteries in a flash light." She laughed at my

naivety.

"Oh. I didn't know that."

"I can see that! My charger is upstairs. It's a little black cord next to

my nightstand. Just plug it into the bottom of the phone, and it should be

good to go in a couple of hours."

"Thanks, mom." I headed upstairs in compliance with her instructions.

"Mr. Mitchell raised a good point. Instead of walking home, why didn't you call me?" Mom asked.

I couldn't believe what I was hearing! Was she really siding with him?!

"I told you, mom. I forgot you had even given me a phone! I never use the phone at home! Why would I use a cell phone? You're the only person I call. Ever." I responded with a snip. To me, it was common logic. Too bad nobody else saw it that way.

"So he gave you detention the rest of the week?" She asked.

"Yeah, and its crap! I don't think it's fair!" I whined, wanting her to alleviate my detention load.

"Well, I think it'll serve as a good reminder. Maybe next time, you'll remember to call me for help instead of trying to fix it yourself by cutting classes." Mom verbally slapped me in the face.

"Thanks, mom." I sneered as I squeezed the phone.

"Anything else?" She asked cheerfully.

"Nope. Bye." I said, slamming the 'talk' button. The phone responded, cutting the call short. Attaching the lavender device to the cord, I stormed into my room. I needed someone who would listen to me, so I ran to the

only entity that I knew who would.

October 28, 2006 4:11 pm

I cannot believe her! She's taking his side! My mom thinks Mr. Mitchell is right! That I should've called her for help instead of walking home! They both agree that since I have a cell phone that I should've called someone for help! Um, excuse me! I never use the house phone! Using a phone to call someone when I barely use it didn't occur to me! Apparently, that doesn't matter! Fucking assholes! I'm serious! If one more bullshit thing happens, I'm going to explode! I can't take this! It doesn't matter what I do! I'm always wrong! It doesn't matter if I make a mistake! It's the end of the world! Fuck this shit! I can't take much more!!

Chapter 30

Anger grew inside of me with each passing hour. The earth continued
to rotate as the hours passed, and my emotions took advantage of growing
during the night. By the arrival of the sun, I was blinded by rage.

You know you are right, Id whispered. *You didn't do anything wrong,
and those sons of bitches are just out to get you.*

*Hey, now! They have a valid point! All they're asking is that you ask
for help! They want to help you, but how can they help if you don't speak
up and tell them that something is wrong?* Superego tried to placate to my
sense of decency, but it was waning.

*And when I ask for help, they don't think that what's bothering me is
serious. If they're not going to take me seriously, then what incentive do I
have to ask anyone for help?* I snapped back. I was done listening to the
logical, caring side of myself. It had gotten me nowhere except deeper and
deeper into trouble.

I'm glad you're starting to see things my way. Id smiled.

Please, listen to me! You don't want to hurt anyone! Superego pleaded.

And I suppose it doesn't matter that I'm hurting? I asked rhetorically.

"Rise and shine, sleepyhead." Mom smiled as she flicked the switch. The light blinded me, making me unaware of her immediate presence.

"I <u>am</u> up." I snapped.

"Aren't you going to get ready for school?" She asked.

"I was just going throw on some pajamas." I lied. I had no intention of going to school just to rot in detention, but I knew she wouldn't understand.

"Okay. Do you want a ride?" She smiled.

"No thanks. I was going to walk."

"Okay. I'll see you downstairs." Standing up, she took her leave in search of continuing her own morning ritual.

Slowly, I rolled out of bed. I had to find trivial events to dwindle her remaining time at home, in addition to giving her the impression that I was really going to school. Heading downstairs, I found a small amount of comfort in my morning cup of sunshine.

"Don't forget, dear. You have to testify at the trial tomorrow." Mom reminded me.

"Are you going to call me into school? I don't want them giving me more detention for legitimately missing detention!" I sneered.

"Somebody's in a grouchy mood!" Mom observed. "I was planning on it."

"Sorry. I'm not trying to be. I just think it's crap." I sighed.

"I'll let the school know." Mom smiled. "Okay, honey. Give me a hug. I'm off to work. You'd better hurry up if you don't want to be late." Wrapping her arms around me, she gave me a pseudo caring expression.

Hollowly, I returned the gesture. As mom walked out the door, I retreated upstairs.

"Have a nice day," She called out to me.

"You too." I responded. Sitting down in front of my computer, I decided to amuse myself with my favorite mindless activity.

So, how are you going to hurt the little bastards? Id grinned.

I don't know if I want to. I just know that I can't take much more. I sighed.

Then don't hurt anyone. Think of alternate things you can do. Maybe you could join a club or an after school activity. Superego's face lit up in a hopeful attempt to dissuade me from Id's argument.

You know they're not going to stop until you're gone or until they are. That's how it works. Nothing is going to make them care about how much they hurt you, or how it makes you feel. Id reveled in playing devil's advocate.

I'm just saying, can't you explore every other option before you stoop to that level? She pleaded.

And what options haven't I explored?! I asked to be transferred. I go tell the adults when there's a problem. When they misunderstand something, I try to explain things to them, but they don't listen!! What the hell am I not doing to make things better? I snapped.

Maybe they know something you don't know. Maybe they've been there themselves, and they know it's only temporary. Superego held onto the same hollow smile.

And I say if you hook up a sealed container of chlorine gas to the air conditioning unit outside the school and lock the doors, they'll drop like flies. It won't take that much gas to make them all very sick. The internet

said it only takes 430 parts per million. That means for every 1 million

atoms of oxygen, it only takes 430 out of 1 million to be lethal. That's not

a lot, considering the ratio. It would only take a couple of bottles of

chlorine bleach and ammonia cleaner to make enough gas to kill them! By

the time they realize what's going on, it'll be too late. Id squealed, lighting

up at the possibilities.

You shouldn't do that! That will cause mass panic! People will hurt

each other trying to get to safety! Superego was becoming frantic.

Then, I suppose I should lock the doors to avoid people stampeding out

of the school. An evil smile tugged at the left corner of my mouth.

That's my girl. Id returned the smile.

Then, it's settled? I asked.

No! Superego screamed.

Yes. If they don't stop pushing, then push back. Id nodded.

October 29, 2006 8:42 am

Yeah, I know. I'm skipping school. I don't care anymore. Why the fuck

should I go to school, when all I'm going to do is go to detention? And

WHY do I have detention? Because apparently, the adults are dumb asses

and think I was trying to use my phone. I don't need to go to school every

day if I'm only going to get shit on by everyone. Besides, how can anyone

expect me to concentrate and get an education when I always get

distracted with this crap?? Tomorrow is the trial. Well, the part where I

testify. I hope the bitch fries! I hope she gets a nasty jail sentence and she

cries! That'll teach her!! Hahahahahahaha! We'll have to see. As for right

now, I'm going to go back to sleep.

Chapter 31

It was as if someone had reset the speed to which I operated. While the world functioned at normal capacity, fear possessed me to move slower, more labored. Every movement was an agonizing chore.

My hair went bone straight as the brush released the follicles from its embrace. Snarl after snarl, up, down, up, down. I repeated the mindless motions until an outside force snapped me back to reality.

"How long are you going to brush your hair?" Mom laughed.

"Huh? Oh, sorry." I blushed, dropping my arm to my side.

"Come on, honey. We have to get going. The trial starts at 9am, and it's 8:15am. We don't want to be late."

"But I don't know what to wear!" I protested, trying to extend the remaining time.

"What about that little red dress with the black sweater over it? I think that would be cute, and professional." She smiled. I had no idea what she put in her coffee that gave her the ability to be cheery every morning. If offered, I think I'd have to pass on experiencing the same feeling.

"Okay. What about shoes?" I asked, scuttling to my room.

"Wear your black boots. It snowed a little bit last night, and they'll keep your feet warm. Sneakers won't look professional."

"Did you call the school?" I asked, pulling the dress off the hanger.

"Over an hour ago." She called from her room.

"Thank you." I called back.

"You're welcome."

I shook my head. I thought our way of communicating was humorous. I yell to her, she yells to me, and yet neither one of us can go to the other and have a face to face conversation at a reasonable decibel level. What was the world coming to?

"Here's your phone, kiddo." Mom dropped the leash into my purse.

"Thanks. I must have forgotten about it." My voice was muffled by the black turtleneck sweater.

"Okay. Come on. Let's go. I don't want to be late." Mom rushed us to the car as she drove us to our awaiting fate.

As the car rolled forward in silence, my entire body screamed and protested against the treatment incurred by the adults. Did I really have to

testify? What was it going to be like? What the hell was going on?
Logically, I understood that I needed to recount the events from that day in
my own words. Logically, I knew that I wasn't to blame for what the
cheerleader decided to do, and that she was the individual who had to face
the consequences to her actions.

Emotionally, I was a train wreck. I wanted to run and scream and hide.
I didn't want to confront trouble. I wanted it to look for me, and not find
me, as I cuddled under some large mass that made me invisible.

In silence, we made our way up the elevator to the second floor.

"I thought Cindy was on the third floor." I said, dumbfounded.

"She is, but the courtroom is on the second floor. That's where we're
meeting her." Mom replied.

"Oh." I nodded.

"Now, don't forget honey. Just go up there, and tell the truth. Don't
embellish, and don't lie. You have nothing to be ashamed of or feel
embarrassed about. You didn't do anything wrong, and the judge is only
interested in the honest facts." She smiled, rubbing my shoulders.

"Okay." I nodded, exhaling loudly. My breathing became labored as the elevator doors opened. I was getting more and more nervous as the milliseconds passed. *At this rate, I'll completely lose my mind in a matter of minutes!* I thought.

Walking into court, I clung to the protectiveness of my mother's bubble. I could see the cheerleader sitting at the table on the right side of the court room with a man, and I saw Cindy sitting at the table on the left side of the court room.

"Hey." Cindy whispered to us.

Before we could respond, a deep voice bellowed, "All rise! Now presenting the Honorable Judge Dominic Gherk."

What? Did he just call the judge a jerk? Superego asked incredulously.

Let's see if he is a jerk. He'd better find the bitch guilty. Id shrugged.

Looking around the room again, I saw Sgt. Saroka sitting in a pew built for the audience. With a slight nod, he greeted me. I nodded back, extending the same greeting. There were dozens of people sitting in the pews. I didn't recognize almost anyone. Then I saw the fiery glow of auburn curls…

My heart leaped as my eyes made contact with Justin. A giant grin instantaneously spread across my face, and he smiled back.

Oh, I'm so glad he showed up to support you! See? I told you he was a friend and that you could trust him! Superego beamed.

"Now calling to the stand, Ms. Robin Edwards." The voice bellowed again.

Whipping my head around, I mimicked a deer caught in the headlights. Did he really just call me to the witness stand? Was I going to have to testify, right now?

Slowly, I stood up and inched my way over to the witness box.

"Do you swear to tell the truth, the whole truth, and nothing but the truth, so help you god?" He quoted, shoving a bible in front of me.

"Yes." I mumbled, taking my seat. Gracefully, the bailiff returned to the side of the courtroom.

"Now, Ms. Edwards, can you tell us the events of the morning of October 9, 2006?" Cindy stood up and approached my box.

I looked at her blankly, unsure of what to say.

"It's okay, dear. Don't be afraid. October 9th was the day that you allegedly received an injury at the hands of the defendant." She smiled.

Nodding, my brain had quickly caught up. Now I knew which morning she was referring to. That was the day that bitch shoved me into my locker!

"Well, I went to my locker at lunch time. I always go to my locker at lunch time to get my afternoon books. That way, I don't have to carry all of my books all day long. I carry my morning books in the morning and my afternoon books in the afternoon." I was beginning to ramble. I always rambled when I got nervous. I couldn't help it. Everyone was staring at me! Was there nothing else they could possibly be looking at?

"Go on." She smiled again, glancing at the judge. I glanced over at the jury box. It was empty.

"Well, I was taking my morning books out of my book bag when someone pushed me. I hit the inside of my locker right here." I pointed to the still healing scab on my eyelid.

"Do you know for certain who pushed you?" She asked.

"No, but when I looked, I saw a bunch of cheerleaders walking down the hallway, laughing." I responded.

"Have you had encounters with the defendant before this incident transpired?"

"Yes. Her locker used to be next to mine. She would always kick my books, or slam it shut. Things like that." I shrugged.

"To this day, have you ever done anything mean to her?"

"No."

"So, your testimony is that you never kicked her books and you never pushed her or slammed her locker shut? That when she pushed you into your locker, it was an unprovoked, preemptive strike against you?"

"Yes."

"Have you ever yelled at her, taunted her, or said mean things to her?" Cindy asked, raising an eyebrow.

"No!" I exclaimed. "Never!"

"Thank you. I'm done with this witness." Cindy walked back to the table and sat down next to mom. Mom mouthed "Great job!" and smiled at me.

Now it was the defense's turn. He was a bitter, morose man who wore a flat suit to match his flat affect.

"Good morning." He spoke. His voice eerily echoed in the silent courtroom, causing an icy chill to run down my spine.

"Good morning." I politely responded.

"According to your testimony, you never did anything to provoke my client? You never put your books in the way of her locker, making her late to class?" He asked in the same icy tone.

"No. Never." I shook my head.

"And you never teased her?" He asked.

"No." I kept shaking my head.

"Did you ever say anything nice to my client?" He asked, raising his voice at the end.

"No. I left her alone." I said, blinking.

"So, you weren't nice, but you weren't mean. Is that what you're saying?"

"I guess." I shrugged.

"And you never actually saw my client push you into your locker?" He asked.

"No." I responded quietly.

"No further questions." He sat back down.

As I stood up to escape back to the bubble of my mother, I heard the judges' voice float down to me.

"Excuse me, Ms. Edwards. Did anybody say anything to influence your testimony here today?" He asked gently.

"Yes." I replied, frozen in a half standing position.

"And who influenced your testimony?" His voice was still gentle, as if he knew he was dealing with a skittish rabbit.

"My mom." I pointed.

"And what did your mother say?" He asked.

"She told me to tell the truth, and not to lie or embellish. She said that you were only interested in the honest facts." I disclosed the details of the conversation mom and I had in the elevator.

A couple of people snickered in the courtroom. What was so funny?

"Okay. Thank you. You may return to your seat." With a big smile, he excused me.

"You are such a dork!" Mom laughed at me as I sat down.

"What? What'd I do?" I asked, bewildered.

" 'Yeah, my mom told me to tell the truth.' You are priceless!" She laughed at me. I rolled my eyes at her.

"All rise." The bailiff called. As we stood, the judge retreated out the side door.

"What's going on?" I thought.

"The judge is going to review the evidence, and make a decision." Cindy informed us.

"How come the jury box is empty?" I pointed.

"The defendant's parents decided they wanted the judge to decide the outcome, and not a jury." She replied.

"Oh." I said. "Is she going to testify?"

"No. Her lawyer didn't think it would help her case." Cindy shook her head.

"Is anybody else going to testify?" I asked.

"Everybody else already testified." Mom replied.

"Oh." Who knew a one syllable answer could be so efficient?

Looking back at Justin, I smiled hopefully at him. His smile was hollow, and it rang an alarm inside my soul. Furrowing my brows as if to ask "what's wrong?", he shook his head at me.

"All rise." The bailiff yelled, startling me. As everyone stood, we ushered in the quiet judge.

"You may be seated." He said, organizing the paperwork he brought with him.

Everyone went dead silent, awaiting his decision.

"It is the opinion of the court that this was a preemptive, unprovoked attack perpetrated by the defendant." He began.

"While the victim admits to not having seen the defendant actually commit the crime, the other members present at the time of the attack confirm it was the defendant, and the defendant alone, who acted without cause.

"With that said, the court finds the defendant guilty of gang assault in the third degree, and is sentenced to spend 5 years in a minimum security facility, with eligibility for parole after 3. The court is adjourned." The judge banged his gavel.

Fry, bitch, fry! Id squealed. *Justice has been served!*

Poor thing. Superego cooed.

A smile crossed my face as mom and Cindy hugged me unanimously.

"Where do you want to go to celebrate, kiddo?" Mom grinned at me.

"I don't know. Where do you want to go?" I asked.

"I don't know, but let's go celebrate!" Happiness beamed from every orifice of her being.

"Hold on. Let me go say hi to Justin." I jogged over to him, glancing at the cheerleader. Her parents were trying to console her as she cried in their arms. I felt a twinge of pity for her, but it was too fleeting to make a difference.

"Hey, you made it." I smiled at him.

"I said I would be here." He snapped at me.

"What's wrong?" I asked, puzzled.

"I can't believe you! You really don't get it, do you?" His anger consumed his beautiful eyes, giving them a dangerous quality.

"No…"

"They just convicted my sister!" He fumed.

"What?" My eyes bulged in disbelief.

"That's fucked up! My sister 'accidentally' bumps into you, and now she has to go to jail! That's bullshit! You are such a bitch!" He spun around on his heels, rushing over to his family.

It was as if he reached into my chest and ripped out my heart. I stood there, unable to regain any composure after he had proverbially slapped me in the face.

"Come on. Let's go." Mom wrapped her arm around me.

"I just want to go home." I ran out of the courtroom as the tears ran down my cheeks.

■■

The rest of the day was spent sobbing in my bed. Mom had pried the information from me, and her only comment was, "I knew there was something wrong with that boy."

Time did nothing to heal the pain of being betrayed. I had waited so long for a friend, and it would take even longer for me to have one. When I was able to lie to myself about having one friend, it made the pain and loneliness a little more tolerable. Now, there was only the truth. I was completely alone. No friends. No one. Just me.

The pain was almost too much to bear. Mercifully, I cried myself to sleep.

My body moved stiffly through the cold, lugging the supplies I carried. My soul remained shattered in pieces on the courtroom floor, and I hadn't been able to retrieve them.

Looking at my left wrist, my watch read 8:17am. *Good. Everyone who's going to be here is already inside.* I thought. Pulling a chain out of the duffel bag, I wrapped it around the bars of the doors and locked the two ends together. *Good luck getting this door to open.* Numbly, I trudged around to the other two doors and chained them up as well. Try as everyone might, there was no way these bad boys were going to open.

Id danced with glee as my hands yanked the a/c tubing off of the generator. Fastening it to an air tight lid, I pushed down to stop any leaks from happening.

Yes! Now put the chemicals into the container, and seal the box shut! Id screamed in anticipation.

Please don't do this. Superego pleas fell on deaf ears.

Brushing my hair out of my face, I pulled out the ammonia bottles. Both hands spun their respective caps off and poured the contents into the plastic storage container.

Good. That looks like enough. Now add the chlorine. Id pranced around like a child on Christmas morning.

No sooner had I picked up the chlorine bleach than an alarm went off in my head.

Make it so that you can put the bleach in, and seal the container as fast as you can. You don't want any of it escaping. You want everyone inside to have all the gas! Id warned.

Arranging the lid and the container within centimeters of each other, I poured all three bottles of bleach in as fast as robotically possible. I could hear the fizz from the reaction, and my head immediately reacted in pain upon contact.

Pouncing on the lid, I heard the plastic edges click as it closed.

Good. Now go to a window. Id commanded.

What window? I waited for a more explicit command.

The biggest one you can think of. Don't you want to watch these bastards drop like flies? Id cackled.

I started walking. The front doors had the largest windows that came to mind, and it was relatively close. It gave me enough time for the gas to kick in.

Patiently, I stood there waiting. No bodies were in sight. I knew it was a matter of time before they would try to escape the horrors that were about to befall them. Checking my watch, it read 8:26am.

It shouldn't be long now. Id grinned.

When I looked up, I saw several frantic pairs of eyes staring at me, pleading for help. There were hands wrapped around their own throats, trying to make the burning stop. I could hear coughing from several people as the greenish yellow vapor settled to the ground.

People started bending forward and began to vomit. Others rubbed their eyes. I kept looking from person to person, enjoying their misery.

"Open the doors! What's wrong with you?!" A panicked feminine voice vociferated.

Rot in hell, bitch! Id fulminated.

My diaphragm emitted a low rumbling laughter as my eyes feasted on the bodies falling to the floor…